MW01251351

PROSE SERIES 75

**Canada Council   Conseil des Arts
for the Arts   du Canada**

ONTARIO ARTS COUNCIL
CONSEIL DES ARTS DE L'ONTARIO

Guernica Editions Inc. acknowledges the support of The Canada Council for the Arts.
Guernica Editions Inc. acknowledges the support of the Ontario Arts Council.

F. G. PACI

HARD EDGE

A NOVEL

GUERNICA
TORONTO — BUFFALO — CHICAGO —LANCASTER (U.K.)
2005

Copyright © 2005, by F. G. Paci and Guernica Editions Inc.
All rights reserved. The use of any part of this publication, reproduced, transmitted in
any form or by any means, electronic, mechanical, photocopying, recording or otherwise stored in a retrieval system, without the prior consent of the publisher is an
infringement of the copyright law.

Antonio D'Alfonso, editor
Guernica Editions Inc.
P.O. Box 117, Station P, Toronto (ON), Canada M5S 2S6
2250 Military Road, Tonawanda, N.Y. 14150-6000 U.S.A.

Distributors:
University of Toronto Press Distribution,
5201 Dufferin Street, Toronto, (ON), Canada M3H 5T8
Gazelle Book Services, White Cross Mills, High Town Lancaster LA1 1XS U.K.
Independent Publishers Group,
814 N. Franklin Street, Chicago, Il. 60610 U.S.A.

First edition.
Printed in Canada.

Legal Deposit — Second Quarter
National Library of Canada
Library of Congress Catalog Card Number: 2005921437
Library and Archives Canada Cataloguing in Publication
Paci, F. G.
Hard edge / F.G. Paci.
(Prose series ; 75)
ISBN 1-55071-212-8
I. Title. II. Series.
PS8581.A24H37 2005 C813'.54 C2005-900848-2

HARD EDGE

I

It was the time of disco, of Donna Summer and Blondie. Of Elaine's and Studio 54, where the celebs blew coke by the pound and went upstairs for some quick sex. Of *Saturday Night Fever* and the Bee Gees. Of the Son of Sam. Soon Elvis would die like some kind of saint. Punk would rise and New Wave would catch on. It was the time of excess and hedonism. The *Playboy* philosophy ruled. Cities like New York were in the grip of urban blight. The subways were covered with graffiti. Muggers and the homeless were everywhere. Times Square was the foyer to a triple-X porn theatre.

Sex, drugs, and rock 'n' roll.

But Lisa and I didn't give a fuck about all that. We were into art, love, and knowledge.

We were walking past the Park Plaza with its limos and ten-thousand dollar rooms and then up Fifth Avenue alongside Central Park, when I felt myself playing Kierkegaard.

I plucked a leaf off a low branch of a tree that came over the parapet.

"This is a leaf," I said. "An oak leaf, to be precise. Look at this leaf."

"Yeah, so what?" Lisa said, giving it a quick glance.

I held the leaf up against the slight breeze.

"Either the wind rustling this leaf," I said, "is just the wind. Or – and this is a mighty *or* – or . . . it's the breath of God."

She looked hard at me, rolled her eyes, and shook her head. "The wind is just the wind, Croach. The leaf is just a leaf."

"So you'd think," I said. "So you'd think."

By New York standards, it was a damn hot summer. The city was choking in a heavy smog. Air Conditioners ran at full blast. Lisa was in her tan khakis and black camisole top, loping beside me in her long strides, smiling, her long brown hair tied up in this intricate way with barrettes. I was carrying our picnic lunch in a knapsack and wearing a white tennis shirt and cut-off jeans.

We were on our way to the Metropolitan Museum and later to see a new idea, Shakespeare in the Park. Except that Shakespeare was over for the summer. He was being replaced by a Greek tragedy. About fathers killing daughters and mothers killing husbands.

Watching Lisa walking in the heavy air, tossing her head back, taking her long strides – head erect, shoulders back – was like imagining St. Joan leading her army against the English.

She was magnificent. No two ways about it.

She had everything. Stunning looks. Intelligence. Personality. A good heart. A total commitment to her chosen vocation. And she was a heathen in bed. The total package.

I felt blessed.

I had first set eyes on her in the dimly lit St. Mark's basilica in Venice. Clad in her usual black outfit, she was a surreal madonna appearing out of the darkness of my Italian past. Our union had been historically consummated when I had shed blood for her in the Roman catacombs, taking her away from her previous boyfriend, Tony Cicerone.

"Remember Tony Cicerone?" I said as we walked. "Whatever happened to him?"

"The last I heard, he was painting in Montreal."

In Rome, on the way to the catacombs and before slicing my arm, Tony had inadvertently given me a mantra that had seeped into my consciousness like new blood: a myth is a lie that tells the truth. As a mythmaker, I could have my cake and eat it too.

Since the Italian trip, years ago, Lisa and I had gone to the Faculty of Education together, got jobs in separate cities, and conducted an inter-city relationship. Teaching gave us three long holidays to meet and catch up on all the sex we had missed. Sometimes she came up to my hometown. More often I went down to Toronto. In between we wrote letters and spoke on the phone, our breaths a poor substitute for the contact of skin.

The past year Lisa got fed up with the pettiness and venality of teaching. This fall she was starting her postgraduate degree in Art History.

"If I get a doctorate at least I can make some money in an atmosphere more conducive to my work," she said. "You'll die as a teacher, Croach. They'll suck the life right out of you."

"I'm mixing with the masses," I told her, with my nose raised to the heavens. "Like Socrates and Kierkegaard. I'm not going to lock myself in an ivory tower like Hegel. Make my philosophy a magnificent mansion that no one can live in."

Since the Italian trip, I had been cultivating a new persona. I was no longer apprehensive about my Italian roots, my peasant father, my inglorious past in my hometown in northern Ontario. I no longer hung my head in shame and felt sorry for myself. I had become proud of who I was, and of the ashes I had risen from. This could only work if I saw myself as the misunderstood artist, strong in his solitary insight and railing against the dim-wittedness of the masses.

After sucking up all the black blood of Wittgenstein, Kierkegaard and Socrates – both masters of indirect communication – had become my newest godfathers. Irony had become my mask with which to face the hostile world.

I hadn't seen this as clearly as I saw it now. All the infusions of black blood from my godfathers and godmothers had given me a role I had always aspired to. Like Kierkegaard, I'd play a comedy in the everyday world.

I brought the oak leaf up again and peered at it as if looking at Yorick's skull.

"Either we live centred on the inside," I said, "or centred on the outside."

Lisa disregarded me.

"If we marry we will regret it," I said, spilling the black blood of my godfather. "If we don't marry we will regret it. If we trust ourselves we will regret it. If we don't trust ourselves we will regret it. If we hang ourselves we will regret it. If we don't hang ourselves we will regret it."

"Oh, stop it, Croach," Lisa shook her head. "Look at that couple over there."

She indicated a horse-drawn carriage passing us on the street with a young couple wrapped in each other's arms. Thinking we were envious of them, they smiled at us and waved.

"How hideous," Lisa said. "I hate that sort of saccharine romantic convention. And taking a taxi instead of walking four blocks," she indicated all the yellow cabs. "And all those rich people across the street who pay an arm and a leg to live separated from the poor and dispossessed."

"Either we lead a rich life, or a poor life . . ."

"You don't have to lead an extravagant life," she said. "Even if they gave half of their possessions away, they'd feel better and feed thousands of people at the same time."

"Either we give up our money or we don't give up our money," I said.

Her face tensed, as if I had issued a challenge.

Up the street she spotted a bag lady camped against the parapet to the park and put a twenty dollar bill in her wooden cigar box. The middle-aged woman, in dirty gypsy clothes who had obviously slept in the park, hardly noticed her. She was looking at the sky in a daze.

"You didn't have to do that," I said, grabbing her by the shoulders. "I was only kidding."

"Piet Mondrian lived on sardines in Paris for ten years," she said, curt and hot. "Either you talk or – and this is a mighty *or* – you act."

We resumed walking. She was in deep thought. I looked over the parapet and spotted the ponds, the lawns, the shaded woods where people were resting in the park.

At the museum vendors had their wares on the cobble-stones. A young man who had painted himself into a silver statue stood immobile behind his donation box. A huge banner hung over the entrance, highlighting the present exhibition.

We sat down on the edge of the fountain close to the front steps and waited to see the statue flinch. Sweat was trickling down his legs.

"I'm beginning to worry about the fall, Croach," she looked up to me with her large eyes. "What's going to become of us in the fall? I don't know if I can stand another separation. I'm tired of just meeting during our vacations."

I didn't know what to say. We remained in awkward silence.

"We have to go forward, Croach. We can't keep going like this. Meeting in neutral places. We have to do something else."

The statue-boy, harassed by a group of kids, finally shook his head and told them to fuck off.

Inside, it was cool and cavernous. We quickly went through the armour room, saw all the instruments of war, then the Egyptian rooms, the Eastern artwork, and quickly got to the European art on the second floor, where the Rembrandts were.

Lisa studied the self-portrait, done in 1660, nine years before his death. It showed all of the artist's age in the decay of his face.

I wandered over to another room and saw something that caught my eye. David's *The Death of Socrates*, painted in 1787. It showed Socrates sitting up in bed, reaching for the cup of hemlock with one hand while the other was raised in discourse. His pupils were arranged around him in various states of incomprehension and grief.

Look carefully, Kierkegaard whispered in my ear: our mentor. He chose the hemlock. It's either the hemlock or the cross.

By the time we finished with the museum it was late afternoon. We slipped into the park behind the massive building, went under a small bridge close to the obelisk, and headed for the Great Lawn and the theatre. A long line had already formed for the free tickets. Later, we sat on the grass close to the large pond at the Belvedere castle and had our picnic in the shade of a tree.

"The Rembrandts were fantastic," Lisa said, biting into a sandwich. "De-emphasize the light, put in black, and you make the little light so magical."

"Socrates chose the hemlock. He died a penniless man in the service of the soul."

"Great for Socrates. Oh, Croach, the Rembrandts have revived my spirits. If only I could see them whenever I want?"

All the artwork in the museum – the Italian and Spanish masters, the Flemish and French galleries, the impressionists, Lisa's Rembrandts, and David's *Death of Socrates* – had made my eyes weary.

I felt sticky with sweat. Luckily a mild breeze came up. We could see the skyline of the Upper West Side over the trees. The sun had sunk over the park.

Two young girls, no more than twenty, both in loose summer dresses, were sitting on the grass facing each other and brazenly smooching in front of everyone.

"Look at that," I said.

"Have you ever made love to a man, Croach?" she said.

"What?"

"I have. With a woman, that is."

She laughed when she saw my expression.

Some time ago she had told me about all her previous lovers. It started with this art teacher in Montreal who was much older. He had taught her how to please men. She had been an avid learner. Then there had been the art school crowd. Then the guys at the Commune where she had met Manda Farrell, my previous girlfriend. Since our Italian trip she had professed to be faithful. There had been plenty of offers, she told me, and it had been hard to resist so many guys, but once she was with a guy she was with a guy.

"Oh, Croach," she put her face on my chest, "I didn't know what I wanted back then. I was young and I tried to please everyone. Doing it with a girl didn't mean anything.

She was my best friend, and we had a brief fling. I was a wild hedonist back then. But now I'm finished with all that, Croach. Believe me. But you have to know me. You can't love me unless you know me."

I remained silent. Love was too big a word for me. I admired her. Found her fascinating. Found her beautiful and exciting to be with. I could speak to her about anything. And she understood.

"Croachy?" she said, her voice tender.

I talked about Kierkegaard's second stage in life's way, the *or* stage. The ethical life over the sensuous aesthetic life of the seducer. We had to be responsible, according to Judge Wilhelm. Make lasting engagements. Choose duty and commitment. Pain to pleasure. To make things last.

She listened with a little smile. "What're you saying, Croach? Are you making a proposal or are you judging me?" She laughed.

"Neither/nor," I said. I was only playing. Playing a part. Counterfeiting an emotion where there wasn't any. And I was sweating.

"Are you proposing, Croach?"

"I don't know what I'm saying," I looked at my watch. "You don't want to get married anyway. You don't want kids, you've told me often enough."

"Well . . ." she said. "You can get married and not have kids, you know."

I sat up. "The play's going to start."

Later, as we were watching the Greek tragedy in the open air theatre, her body was stiff beside me. The chorus was very impressive. All those voices joining and creating a massive human wail against the night sky. The gods had set limits on human action. Agamemnon had sacrificed his daughter Iphigenia. He had spilled the blood of his own kin. He had to pay with his life. But I recalled in *Fear and Trembling* how Kierkegaard had compared Abraham to Agamemnon. They had both done their duty out of faith.

And then there was Cassandra, captive princess of Troy, who had been given the gift of prophecy by Apollo but was doomed to suffer the anguish of not being believed. No matter what mask she put on, her cries were ignored. This was certainly my lot, I had whispered to Lisa.

When I regarded her proud profile against the New York skyline, I wondered if I was as doomed as Agamemnon. Our first year together I was constantly apprehensive about satisfying her sexually. I had only been with one other woman, Manda, and that had been brief. I had read *Playboy* and other 1960s magazines and books about the sexually liberated woman. The woman of the 1970s needed orgasms. And Lisa had been with many men, not to mention her girlfriend. The pill had brought out the sexually voracious woman who had been lurking underneath the surface for millennia, according to some of my godfathers. She could orgasm five, six times.

After we had made love I'd say, "Was that all right?"

One time she got mad and gave me a lecture.

"Quit it! It's not about cuming or not. The more I get used to you, the more enjoyable it is. It's not mechanics and gymnastics. Don't separate things, Croach. It's all one. It's about love and intimacy."

2

It was late morning. Lisa and I were still in bed. The midtown traffic noise competed with the whir of the air conditioner. The hot light slanted through the Venetian blinds.

We were in an old hotel between the St. Moritz and the Essex House in Central Park South. The room was small and seedy-looking, smelling of old carpet. A faded watercolour of the Brooklyn Bridge hung over the bed.

"It's tacky, yes," Lisa said when I first saw it. "But it has a certain old world charm to it. At least it's not hideous."

Hideous was one of her favourite words. It could be a modern glassy highrise or a subdivision of townhomes. It could be a rundown tenement or the ritzy Pierre Hotel on Central Park East. Hideous didn't only mean ugly to look at, but fake, pretentious, extravagant, luxurious, unjust, inauthentic. Hideous was close to evil. Lisa's artist's eyes were tempered with social justice. Her parents had been card-carrying Communists. She had been raised to be sensitive to any injustice, whether it was the plight of workers or the treatment of the homeless.

Except she wasn't political. She was an artist. She found the state-funded stilted art of the Soviet Union as hideous as anything. She realized that art, in its authentic meaning, and politics, especially the collective Communist politics of the Soviet Union and China, didn't mix. Art didn't serve the interests of a tyranny, whether it was left or right, she said. Art served no vested interests. It was free. It was uncompromising, she said. Even the Renaissance masters, who were patronized by the Church and various tyrants of the city-states, painted what they were supposed to paint on the surface, yes, but painted with their true blood underneath. They had an underlying agenda. Art broke free of all constraints. It was the expression of the human spirit in all its grandeur and in all its squalidness, she said.

This I understood from my friend, Gene Marinelli, who was a disciple of Allan Bloom. The great authors of the past had an esoteric significance that most people were blind to. It was hidden communication. Bloom had translated Plato and certainly knew Socrates better than most people.

Such beliefs were important to Lisa. She could joke about them. She could laugh at herself. But she was deadly serious. Art was her religion, as simple as that.

Whenever I became maudlin about art she quoted Baudelaire. The artist was responsible to no one but himself. He gives to the future centuries only his own work. He dies without children. He is his own king, his own priest, his own god.

We talked about these matters all the time. Some things we agreed on. Some things we didn't agree on.

What we were always questioning, however, was whether we had genuine talent.

"I don't know, Croach. I don't know," she'd say to me often. "I don't know if I have it."

She had a number of exhibitions. Some people – teachers, critics, and so on – had told her she was good. But good wasn't good enough to Lisa. If she was going to devote her life to art, she had to be damn good.

"It's doubly, triply hard for a woman," she said. "Name one female artist before 1900."

"I don't know," I said.

"There were a few, but are they showing in any notable museum or gallery? In writing at least you have Austen, Eliot, George Sand, Shelley, and the Brontës. But did any of them have kids? Someone like Emily Carr had to give up everything for her work. Even now, for a woman, it's either her work or a family. She can't have both. She wants to get a show anywhere and the dealers ask her if she can produce a body of work for a certain time. You can't do that with kids."

Emily Carr was her heroine, Lisa told me way back. Emily Carr had done it. Lisa had read and re-read Carr's books. Carr had given up not only kids, but a husband. Lisa, however, liked sex too much to give up men.

"If I ever had a child," she said, "that would be the end of my art. I'd devote my total time to the child. I couldn't do anything less. You can't have a child and be an artist, a serious artist, at the same time. Not for a woman, anyway."

Lisa continually told me how her own parents left the Communist Party to have her, their only child. Once she was born they had devoted their whole life to her.

I had met her parents on a number of occasions. They had an apartment at Eglinton and Yonge, close to the subways, shops, and libraries of a trendy area. They were both retired, in their sixties, and white-haired, showing me a reserve that I didn't know how to interpret. Until Lisa told me that they were always aloof with her boyfriends. I added one and one and came up with the answer. Why get serious with one boyfriend, when there could be another the next day?

Her parents were more like friends to her now, she told

me. They had backed her artistic ambitions all the way. She was their whole life now. Whatever she wanted, she got. When she moved to Montreal to do her undergraduate studies at Concordia, they had come with her. When she moved back to Toronto, they came with her. She still lived with them, though she had her own studio space on Queen Street, in a warehouse floor she shared with a couple of other artists.

Lisa started to trail her tongue along my moist abdomen.

"Let's not get up yet," she said in her baby-girl voice. "Can't you feel the energy in the air? New York gets me so excited. Isn't the little piggy ready yet?"

I waited, holding my breath.

"This little piggy went to market," she said, holding my big toe. "This little piggy stayed home. This little piggy had roast beef. This little piggy had none . . ."

"Hey, we have to get those Broadway tickets," I said.

I could smell the sticky wetness of the sheets and her body.

Her dark eyes stared at me in the shadowy light like a playful animal.

"What tickets?" she feigned ignorance and propped herself up against the pillows. The faint light made an indistinct shadow of her head and shoulders against the wall. "We haven't finished playing, have we? Doesn't your little piggy want more?"

"We have to get those tickets if you want to see the play."

She pouted, rolling onto her back. "Tired of my body already?"

I sat up and contemplated her.

She was just a little shorter than me. With a flat stomach and long legs that made her walk in loping strides. She was a hiker and wore her trekking boots in the city. She could walk for miles without losing pace. I had trouble keeping up with her. With one knee slightly upraised, the soft milky skin of her inner thighs was exposed. Her straight brown hair rested on her shoulders. Her long face with the high forehead was as milky and smooth-featured as her inner thighs. As she blinked in mock hurt, I caught her darting dark eyes. As attractive as she was, she didn't know vanity. She was a vision of desire and composure. A work of art as fine as I had ever seen.

The sight of her got me going again. "You want to play, uh?" I said.

I inched down the bed and put my face close to the dark tuft of hair between her legs, which stood out against her milky skin. In the stifling air her sex odour was strong and sharp.

My hand reached up to cup her breast. She sighed. But when I nuzzled up to them, they gave off a doughy yeasty odour.

Lisa didn't like using perfume or deodorant. "I don't believe in them," she told me. "The natural odour of the body should be the only allure. You shouldn't need enhancements or false smells, Croach. To present yourself as you truly are, as Emily Carr said countless times. On both the inside and the outside."

I had needed women so much before the Italian trip that I felt I had to make up for a lot of lost time. My insatiable hunger could easily cut through any inconvenient smells. Like the first time Lisa and I made love. It was after our trip to the Vatican, of all places. It had been a warm day in early October and we had both reeked of B.O. But that only seemed to inflame our desire.

"If we're late for the tickets," she said, as she basked in my homage to her body, "we can get them tomorrow. We make our own schedule, Croach. Don't forget the major purpose of this trip."

We had come to New York to see the art galleries, but to screw our brains out as well.

If you believed the talk-show hosts, New York was a cesspool of crime.

"You just have to be careful," Lisa told me. "At night we should take a taxi. But not crosstown. Just up and down the avenues. That's the longest distance. We avoid Central Park and the subway at night. We keep our valuables at the hotel. We stay away from certain areas."

She had been here before, alone and with other boyfriends. She had made the arrangements for the room. Her Artist's Hideaway, she called it.

After we taxied in from Kennedy in the evening and checked in, we had taken a stroll to Times Square. It was just after the theatres had disgorged their audiences. Seeing it for the first time, I was awed by the blazing light. The large Coke sign in the most prominent location. The great masses of neon ads. The theatres. The stores. The porn shops. The sleazy sex shows. The crossroads of show biz, sexual licence, the media, tourism, and the general craziness of the times. Glitz and hustle and fortune. All that New York and the kingdoms of the world had to offer.

We had seen the makeshift booth for half-price tickets. Lisa noticed that Al Pacino, one of her favourite movie actors, was starring in a new play. We decided after Shakespeare in the Park to line up the next afternoon and see what Broadway had to offer.

After a while I could see I wasn't going to get it up so quickly. I needed more time. My head was still in a daze from the sex of last night. I lay back on the bed and stared at the ceiling, breathing heavily.

"Tell me that you're happy with me," Lisa said, changing to a husky tender tone.

"Of course I am. But I'm basically an unhappy person."

After a long pause she said, "How can you possibly be unhappy?"

"I used to be sick in the body. Now I'm sick in the soul."

"You're sick in the head, that's where you're sick at," she said.

"I'm serious."

"What do you have to be sick about?" she said.

"Either you believe in the world, or you believe in God."

"That's bullshit."

Lisa was an atheist. She didn't believe in any God. Not the God of the Bible. Not the God of the Koran or the Brahman of the Vedas. Not the God of the theologians and philosophers. To her God was a myth to justify the exploitation of the powerful. Or to offer us a crutch of solace in the face of a reality we were too cowardly to confront. We had talked about this often. She was adamant. It wasn't a game to her.

As for me, I wasn't so sure. I considered myself a seeker, unwilling to believe all the old myths were total lies. Like Kierkegaard, I believed we were more than rational beings.

But what Lisa said made a lot of sense. And her very character backed it up. She was the kindest, most considerate person I had ever known. She didn't have an unkind bone in her body. While we so-called God-centred religious adherents were brought up to be good for fear of some form of punishment or in the hope of attaining eternal reward, Lisa was good period. To her being good was being considerate and respectful of others before oneself.

When I asked her what she hoped to gain by being good, she looked at me as if the question had never occurred to her.

I remembered how the priests and nuns had given me the impression that we were superior to all other religions. And the fear of eternal damnation that they instilled in us at such a young age.

Lisa made mockery of those priests and nuns.

But if I asked her how she could be so sure there was no God, she'd say, "How do we know there's no Santa Claus?"

I nodded, silenced by the conviction in her eyes.

The inflection in her voice as she stared at me on the bed, waiting for me to get hard again, told me I was in for a little chastisement.

"Bullshit, bullshit, bullshit," she said.

"Could you be a little more succinct, please," I raised my eyebrows.

"You give me a choice when there is no choice."

"If there's no God," I said, feeling the words arranging themselves as in a script, "then what we see and touch and taste is the only reality. If there's no Absolute, then the outer world triumphs. Everything's permitted. And power, followed by pleasure, are the governing principles of life."

"Yeah, sure, so that we're all inherently evil or depraved, right? Which any fool can see is a vicious circle. The religions emphasize how evil we are so that they can offer themselves as the solutions."

We went on in this vein for a while. I tried to play the part of Socrates, but it wasn't easy since Lisa was all too aware of my deceits. When it came down to it, she said, it was how she was raised. Her parents didn't believe in God. Her uncles and aunts didn't believe in God. Interestingly enough, however, they did celebrate Christmas. They thought that every child deserved a Christmas. Since she and Robbie, her cousin, were only-childs, they were spoiled rotten.

"Let me tell you how far it got," she said. "When I told my mom that I had started my period, my parents celebrated the occasion with a party. Can you believe it? I was eleven or so and very embarrassed, to say the least. They invited their former Communist friends. These were the people who campaigned for Fred Rose, the Communist member of parliament, marched to protest the execution of the Rosenbergs, and backtracked on the Soviet invasion of Hungary. Then backed Castro. I slunk away in the corner of the apartment, trying to make my body invisible."

Lisa shook her head.

"Ah, a period," I said.

"Shut up," she said, grabbing my limp cock so hard I yelped in pain.

"Hey, watch it!"

Then she softly cuddled me and took me in her mouth for a while.

"I've often wondered," I said.

"What?"

"What's it's like. To have a period, I mean."

"You wanna be a woman?"

"No."

"You have uterine-envy?"

"No."

"You think we're some sort of alien species, don't you?"

"Yes," I laughed. "I need to do more research into the

female of the species. I could never say I knew human nature till I knew the female of the species."

"Don't you dare," she said, making a feint to hurt me. "Though if I look at things objectively it would do you a world of good, Croach. You definitely have to get women out of your system before you settle down. I know. I've been there."

"You giving me the green light?" I looked at her.

"Stop it."

"C'mon."

"Seriously, though," she looked away, "I don't know how I'd react if you ever did. I don't wanna swell your head even more than it is, but you're a totally new experience for me, Croach. I've never felt for anyone like I feel for you. So I don't know how I'd react."

I let her words settle a bit.

"You know," she said afterwards, "the promiscuous bohemian life isn't all what's it made out to be. I got rather tired of it fast, as a matter of fact. When I see all these older artists, all drunks or lost souls, trying to live at the end of their nerves, I feel sad for them. You can do that when you're young, but you reach a certain age and see it's not worth it. You'd have to be a Francis Bacon, flamboyant and proudly homosexual. You'd have to make your life strikingly original. A god unto yourself. But I'm not up to it any more."

"What're you saying, Lisa?"

"We have to change our arrangement. I can't live in separate cities anymore, Croach."

"We'll live in the same city. A job should open up next year."

She paused and gave me a leery look. "You have any girlfriends up in the Soo?"

"Of course not."

"It's not easy, Croach. I know. If you ever did have a fling, you'd let me know, right?"

"I'm not going to have a fling."

"Oh, the piggy likes me to be hard on you, don't you, little piggy?" she cooed.

I laughed.

I eased up on top of her. She threw her head back against the pillow. Her mouth was open. Her eyes were closed.

3

We were in the theatre to see *The Basic Training of Pavlo Hummel* by David Rabe. The Americans were picking at the scab they called Vietnam.

From the balcony seats we could see someone on the lip of the stage pointing out celebs in the orchestra seats. A few stood up to take bows. They were from the movies, TV, and politics. People who were always in the limelight, indistinguishable from each other.

Kierkegaard was a sort of celebrity in his own day, instantly recognizable on the Copenhagen streets and in the theatres, a stick figure with his umbrella. He was considered a dandy early on in his life, then an object of ridicule. In the small Danish world he moved in, the streets themselves were a theatre where he was constantly on display. Little did they know of his inner life, and his sick soul, and how he was leading them on.

The Broadway theatre itself was intimate, with plush seats and an art-deco charm to it.

Lisa was in her typical black outfit. Fashionable khaki pants and exotic velour top, her long hair flowing down her shoulders. From the outside, she gave the appearance of a cultivated Amazon, proud and sure of herself. It never failed to catch the attention of men. They gave her a second look. Some stared.

It flattered me to be envied by men in suits. Some of these guys would be dealing with millions of dollars on the

New York Stock Exchange the next day. They were suc-
cessful in high-powered finance.

"Isn't New York fantastic?" she whispered, as I kept my
eye on the orchestra seats. "Wouldn't you want to live
here?"

"I don't know."

"Sure, Croach. It's total energy here. For an artist, only
the intense life is worth living."

"I don't know. We'd just be playing at being Americans."

"You play at everything else," she said. "Your sick soul
business, for example."

"That's not playing."

The theatre darkened. Thunderous applause greeted
this little guy in army fatigues. He appeared on the stark
stage bordered at the back with ramps.

"*That's* Al Pacino?" I said.

I couldn't believe he was so small. But all doubts were
dispelled as soon as he opened his mouth. The energy in
his small frame took me by surprise. His words were like
hammer blows. In his rage he spewed slobber over the
stage.

Being about trainees and drill sergeants and such, the
play was quite rough in language. It wasn't anything I
hadn't heard before plenty of times at the steel plant. But
on the stage, with a genteel audience facing these losers, it
was jarring to me.

During my summers I had worked as a labourer in
almost every facet of steelmaking. Even in the Records
Department, where I worked before going to teacher's
college, the guys swore like troopers. During the night
shift they played the radio non-stop. "Ricky, don't dial
that number" and "Don't rock the boat, baby. Rock the

boat" by The Hues Corporation. We processed orders for steel products all over North America.

"He has so much energy," Lisa said after the final bows.

"Much energy, little thought."

She looked at me to see if I was serious. "He's just playing a role," she said.

Later we joined the crowds pouring out of the theatres. Strings of limos were parked curbside. The cabs zoomed crazily through traffic. It was odd to think this was the centre of the show business world. But it was. The dynamo itself. The energy that fed the world American culture. If you can make it here, you can make it anywhere, as the song went.

As we headed back towards the hotel, a gang of black youths in scruffy clothes and Afros came alongside us in a swagger.

"Got any money for some po' blackfolk," one said in a mock singsong.

Lisa went for her handbag and gave them a few loose bills. Later we saw a couple of beggars sleeping on a sidestreet. A young black girl came out of nowhere and stole their Styrofoam cups filled with coins.

"That's so hideous," Lisa shook her head. "There's too wide a gap. The rich close themselves off with their limos and cabs and high-security condos. And the poor have to steal from each other to survive."

"Let's find a place to eat," I said. I was buzzing with ideas after seeing the play.

The corner deli was removed from the more expensive theatre restaurants. We ordered late-night snacks. The red booths were between the windows overlooking the street and a long counter. It was buzzing with talk.

"Where you people from?" a wraith-like waitress asked

us. She had big eyes and gaunt cheeks. Her dark hair was frizzled.

We told her about Al Pacino.

"He came here once," she said in a thick New York accent. "Short, like a runt, right? But he can get into my pants any day."

We looked at her.

"I'm not kidding. I'd spread my legs for him any day."

"These actors," she went on pouring us more coffee, "they're so wound up after a performance, they need something to bring them down. It'd be, like, my contribution to art."

She winked and swished away.

Lisa laughed. "Let's move here right away. Don't you love it?"

"I don't know."

"Everything in the art world is happening here."

"What about Paris?" I said, just for something to say.

"It was Paris once, yeah. But that was a long time ago, Croach. New York took over ever since the days of the Abstract Expressionists."

"We still gotta visit Paris." I was acting cool, detached. A Canadian from a hick town. Totally unrecognized in New York.

"Sure, but this is where the serious artist has to be, Croach."

"Like Andy Warhol, you mean?" I raised my eyebrows.

"Pu-lease," she said. "He's nothing more than a photographer of celebrities now. A total mercenary. The Queen of the Shallows, they call him."

"Who is this 'they?'" I asked her.

"Stop it," she said.

She took out a cigarette and lit up, her movements

studied and precise. She waved away the smoke. We were playing roles in some intellectual play. She could see that men in the deli were looking at her. If some guy ever got pushy and came on to her, I'd probably have to defend her honour.

"Croach," she said a little later, her tone serious, "am I selling out?"

"No."

"Give me the truth. I can take it."

"You're surviving."

"You sure?"

"One step backwards. Two steps forwards."

"I mean, what's the point, if you're not good enough?"

"How can you know? It's too early yet."

"But a professor of Art History – God, I don't know."

"What we both have to do," I said, "is be able to switch from full consciousness to half consciousness. Up and down each day like a yo-yo. Look at me, a twirling dervish of a yo-yo."

She smiled at my efforts to lighten her load. Mixing metaphors. Mixing everything up, like a person who only believed he had mapped a coherent view of the world.

"But painting's different, Croach. It has to absorb the whole being. Though the painter looks for wisdom with her eyes alone, every sense informs those eyes."

"Good, that's good. Keep going."

Unfazed, she went into her full lecture mode.

"The artist sees and feels more intensely than anyone else. Though she lives in poverty she's an aristocrat of sensibility. She fights her culture. She's totally immediate. Totally real. Pure here and now. Pure visions unimpaired by reflection and ideas. Everything in her life is transformed into art. Carr's totems and trees. Pollock's drippings. De Kooning's slashing. Pollock thought of himself as Nature itself. The artist is the last man or woman standing who imitates no one, and realizes their true being."

"Back to nature itself. That's good. Real good."

"You're mocking me?"

"The noble savage, that's good. Rousseau would be proud of that. Pure visions, that's good. Real good."

"Oh, shut up, Croach. Stop it, will you."

"Artists as Christ-figures. Except they wallow in vice and corruption. Screw ups, all of them. Alcoholics. Heroin addicts. Sex fiends."

"Will you quit it. Creativity does strange things to you. How many yo-yo years can anyone take?"

The next day we walked the short distance from our hotel to the Museum of Modern Art on W 53rd Street. It had just been renovated. We slowly went through the various collections. Starting with the first modernists, Van Gogh and Cézanne.

I recognized *Starry Night* immediately. The nocturnal vision of Van Gogh, Lisa said. See how the moon is as bright as the sun, the stars like firecrackers. See how primitive he is. He was a screw-up, yes, but because of his personal screw-ups we have such paintings, she added in a sorrowful tone.

But what attracted me was the *Sleeping Gypsy* of Henri Rousseau. The sleeping negress. The mandolin. The indifferent lion and the dime-store moon. It had a dream-like quality. Like *The Tempest* by Giorgione in Venice. Another enigma that was mesmerizing by its hidden meaning.

Then we went through the cubists, the fauvists, and the surrealists.

"I don't get it," I said, not seeing any coherence anywhere.

"From about 1880 on," Lisa said, "every painter and sculptor was trying to break the shackles of conventional realism. To get behind the surface, so to speak. This was during the advent of photography, of course. As soon as the machine could represent the object, the object could only become a decoration. It was Cézanne, who started to break the tyranny of the flat surface, and Matisse, who brought colour to the forefront, who're considered the initiators of modernism."

"Suppose I write a story about my father," I whispered to her, while the museum strollers were milling around us. "And this story is about what actually happened to him and what possibly could've happened – all mixed up as if it all did actually happen – am I lying or telling the truth?"

"Matisse said that exactitude is not the truth."

When we passed the *Reclining Nude* of Modigliani I grabbed her arm. "That's you! Not exactly you, but you."

"Don't be silly," she laughed. "I shave my armpits."

I looked at it carefully. Except for the smallish breasts, it was definitely Lisa – elongated torso and all.

Later, when we came to the Abstract Expressionists, she lost her light-hearted mood. Her face tensed in studied concentration. We sat in front of a huge wall-size Pollock.

"It's so stupid," I said. All I saw were drips of paint, spurts of colour, haphazard, with no rhyme or reason.

"You don't know," she said. "It looks entirely chaotic on the surface. But you have to see the control in it too. The virtuosity, the intensity of rhythm and depth. It's post-Freudian, of course. Free association. Pure action at the most primitive level. And purely unique, of course."

"Give me a break," I shook my head.

"Look at *Finnegan's Wake*. Don't you want to capture

the immediate experience, Croach? Your true feelings? Your subconscious? Your true self?"

"Sure, but it has to be communicable on some level."

As we walked through the rooms, Lisa studied the works with her trained eye. Sometimes she commented. "I like that." Or, "I don't like that." Sometimes she said, "That's so hideous." I followed her around like a ghostly Dante, getting colour thrown in his face.

One work was the size of the entire wall, and just red. An Ad Reinhardt was just black, all black. And the Warhol soup cans and silkscreens of Marilyn Monroe.

At Willem de Kooning's *Woman 1* Lisa said, "You see how wild and uncontrollable he is."

I saw a medley of slashes and smears, all resembling roughly a woman's body. It looked like something an insane person would do. Her teeth were smiling in hideous disfigurement.

"Another primitive," I said.

We came to Mark Rothko's *Red, Brown, and Black, 1958.* I saw brown and black, but no red. I saw blurred rectangles shading into each other. The rectangles had a certain power and glow to them because of their immense size.

"I don't get it," I said.

"Don't strain. Let the painting speak to you on its own terms."

"*What* terms?"

"Look at the colour," she said with calm patience. "It's as if it's boundless, as if it's all one, each going into the other, separate but one. Rothko thought of himself as very spiritual. These are the great walls of deep silent colours – like the depth of the ocean."

Silence. I couldn't see it. I listened, but I couldn't hear it.

An impeccably dressed older gentleman in a blue blaz-

er and white ascot was studying the huge canvas so carefully I thought he was drowning.

In the room dedicated to de Stijl I saw my first original
Mondrians. Just vertical solid lines, with the primary
colours: red, blue, and yellow. And the three primary non-
colours: white, grey, and black. The *Broadway Boogie-
Woogie* looked like the grid of the city, with syncopated
colours. This, even to the untrained eye, was geometrical,
logical, controlled.

"Mondrian," she said, "and then Ad Reinhardt and
Josef Albers and others were the originators of hard-edge,
the type of art I'm interested in. Geometric forms having
clean boundaries, which generate tension."

Then we went into a large room with Picasso's *Guernica*. The plaque said it was on loan until Spain achieved
democratic freedom. I was bowled over by its size. The
power of the images hammered my eyes. It was all carnage
and horror and dismemberment. The mother was every
mother. The horse was every horse. The dead man on the
ground was every dead man. Even I could see it was an
imitation, as Plato said. It let you re-experience the life-
and-death struggles of other people.

Later, in the outdoors Sculpture Garden, I saw the
huge Rodin sculpture of Balzac and insisted we sit near it.

It rose above the metal chairs.

"I wish you had your camera," I said.

I told her the story of coming upon Balzac's complete
works, all in two special-edition tomes, at the university
library, and my vow to out-write the French master.

"What an idiot I was," I said.

The buildings of Midtown Manhattan rose above the
tight enclosure. People were lazing in the sun around the
cool fountain.

"Whenever I see these great artists," she shook her head, "I feel like an idiot too. I can't stand being mediocre."

We remained silent. I glanced up at the Balzac. He was wrapped in his night shirt. His face was exaggerated, lumpy and powerfully intense. Lisa told me that Rodin exaggerated certain features to give more life. He wasn't after an exact photographic representation. He wanted to depict what the actual couldn't show. Just like the story of my father, she said.

"There's such a vast difference in schools," she said later. "It's all perspective. Everything can be destroyed and reshaped through perspective."

"I'll tell you what I'm trying to see," I fixed my eye on her. "How it's possible that we could be unique and so alike at the same time. The particular and the universal. The finite and infinite at the same time."

"It's called tension," she said. "Speaking of tension, let's get a bite to eat."

We took a taxi to Soho and saw a few private galleries. The old and decrepit warehouses were all windows and Greek columns and fire escapes on their facades. They were just starting to become trendy. The artists displayed were far removed from the Abstract Expressionists. They were mostly descendants of Rauschenberg and Warhol. Post-moderns, Lisa called them. They collected the detritus and garbage of modern culture, glued it together, and framed it. Assemblage, it was called.

"It's not plagiarism," Lisa said. "It's taking certain things out of context and giving them a totally different perspective. When Marcel Duchamp took a toilet seat and framed it, he started a new trend. But that sort of thing can only be done once."

As we were walking north on Broadway, Lisa said, "This is where the New York School started. They were influenced by the Mexican muralists like Rivera, started using large canvases, and needed the large loft space."

We strolled through the Village, with its cafés and clubs. Through Bleeker and Bedford, and came upon Washington Square. It was packed with people around the central fountain close to the arch. On the periphery of the fountain street artists were selling their wares. Canvases. Jewelry. Beads and African batiked cloths. Close to the statue of Garibaldi street performers were plying their trade.

"Have you noticed the statues of famous Italians?" I told Lisa. "The one at Columbus Circle. The Mazzini in Central Park."

She was looking south to the NYU buildings. The sidewalk in front had a long stretch of tables with used books.

"My eyes have taken a beating today," I told her as we rode in a taxi back to the hotel.

"You're such a masochist, Croach," she laughed. "But it's a beating for the better, I'm sure."

That evening we splurged a little and had dinner at a good Italian restaurant across the street from the Lincoln Centre. It had red-brick walls, green-checked tablecloths, and was filled with people attending the evening concert. Across the street we could see the crowds dancing in front of a bandshell in the square.

"Tomorrow we'll do a little sight-seeing, okay. The Guggenheim. The Whitney. Soho."

"What about Yankee Stadium?"

"You're kidding? Baseball?"

"That's New York as much as anything else."

She shook her head as if she knew best. She had been

here before. She was my Virgil leading me down the terraces of the city of the damned. I hoped we would reach the other side of the earth one day, where the mountain would await us.

"When I come to the Soo you can show me your other life," she said.

Later in the year Lisa was supposed to come up to meet my parents. Then it would be me leading her through the caverns of my past, to see from what rough beauty I had sprung.

4

In the next few days Lisa led me through the Whitney and the Guggenheim. We attended a free symphony concert in the park and another concert at the Lincoln Centre. We took a trek through most of Midtown and down to Battery Park and Wall Street where Lisa was very uncomfortable.

"My parents would disown me if they found out I was here. The ultimate symbols of our culture. Some people make a million dollars a day here. It's totally hideous."

Her face scrunched up, as if she were looking at some Hieronymus Bosch demon chewing off the head of another.

"If making money is evil, then everyone's evil," I said.

"You should only make money from honest labour."

She led me through Chinatown and Little Italy, up to Soho and the Village.

We went into a few bookstores. I didn't see anything particularly good. Toronto had better used bookstores, I told Lisa, where I could pick up any Kierkegaard work, as well as the obscure travel books with some of the best prose ever written.

"Who are some of the best English prose writers?" Lisa asked me. "I have to improve my style."

I had seen her reading Greenberg and Rosenberg, the leading art critics of the day, along with Herbert Read and a myriad of anthologies by artists and critics.

I told her about some of my former godfathers of black

blood. Those who sought to mesmerize. Those who sought to picture, without the slightest variation, only what could honestly be said. Those who strove for harmony and balance. Those who played around with form and content.

"Ah, I see," she said. "They all had a unique voice, right?"

"I guess so, yes."

"And how did they break through to that unique voice?"

"I don't know. Are you born with it? Or can you struggle to achieve it?"

"Maybe both, Croach. They weren't afraid to be themselves."

"Okay, fair Virgil, maybe as you're leading me through the city that never sleeps you can lead me to my true self as well."

"I can't work miracles," she laughed.

In our house under the bridge I had been weaned on the old movies on TV about New York. It didn't matter who was in them. Fred Astaire or Doris Day. Cary Grant or Marilyn Monroe. The real star was the city. The island of concrete and dreams. The Big Apple. The Great White Way. New Yoork, New Yoork.

But now, as we walked through 42nd Street, I could see how things had changed. The street had degenerated into sleazy porn theatres and peep shows. Low-lifes and prostitutes choked the sidewalks in the middle of the afternoon. I had kept in touch with my city of dreams through the *New York Times*. After the Knapp Commission hearings police morale was at an all time low. The free flow of drugs was incredible. There was more talk of police corruption in the drug business.

We walked hurriedly through and found refuge in the Public Library at the corner of Fifth Avenue. Upstairs in the display rooms we found an exhibit of Virginia Woolf's manuscripts under glass. I gazed lovingly on the finely wrought handwriting. It was the black blood of one of my godmothers. Had she chosen to be herself right into her early grave?

"Look carefully," I told Lisa. "That's her blood on the page. All dried up."

She shook her head as if I was joking.

In the main reading room later I took out a Woolf novel and read a few pages at random. My loving eyes re-liquefied her dried blood.

"This is what I do," I told Lisa, who held me by the arm. "You see this print? Her consciousness is right in this print. I don't just read it. I caress it with my eyes, I smell it with my nose, and I taste it with my mouth. I bring her back alive. I suck her black blood."

"A Dracula in reverse," she said, looking at me with mock admiration.

"A reverse vampire," I said. "A black-blood sucker."

"Well, I'm gonna start sucking paint then."

"I wanna suck up the whole English language, and spit it out into a thimble," I said.

Next day Lisa told me there was one last must-see before we left New York. It was a new exhibit by a conceptual Earth Artist. I didn't know what she meant. We walked all the way down to lower Soho, to a dirty warehouse with wrought-iron facade. It was a hot day. I was in a white T-shirt and shorts. In her black camisole and tan shorts, her long white legs gleaming in the sun, Lisa looked as if she could step onto any fashion runway.

"What is it?" I said.

"You'll see."

The only indication that it was a gallery was a small plaque at the doorway. We walked up two flights of dingy stairs. The smell of dusty floorboards and rotting wood was combined with new mortar and drywall.

On the third floor a young lady in overalls and pigtails asked us to sign in. I could smell dampness and a pungent odour familiar from childhood. We joined a small group of people down a hallway and through another door, where another young girl in overalls was waiting. She was the last door-keeper of a cast-iron door.

"There's a ten-minute viewing limit," she announced.

I looked at Lisa. Her high forehead held the dim light. She had put on some scent. Not perfume, but bathwater or something. "What's the matter, Croach?" she said. "Afraid to go through?"

A sign indicated the exhibit was called *The Silence of the Earth*.

When it was our turn we stepped out onto a wooden make-shift balcony that overlooked a single room.

The floor was completely covered with soil. Black soil. It was about a foot thick. The bare white walls had track lighting so that we could see the soil in various colours and intensities of light.

My eyes adjusted to the light and colour changes. Lisa was scrutinizing the soil. As if each granule of earth was a word that held the answer to the mystery.

My only thought, besides my surprise, was: How did they get the stuff inside the building?

"This and Performance Art are the leading avant garde stuff now," Lisa whispered, breaking the silence. "This Earth Artist wants a direct confrontation with outside reality."

"Artist?" I said.

A bell rang. Our time was up.

In another hallway we saw the photographs of how the soil was brought in. They showed a truck outside on the street and bags of earth being lifted by a crane through the large windows.

Later we walked up Soho past Houston, to the Village, up McDougall, and turned west to Eighth Avenue. The trendy cafés and restaurants gave way to thrift shops and older decrepit stores.

"It's all a sham," I said, gesticulating wildly as we avoided real New Yorkers. "These people are supposed to have talent? Come on? Andy Warhol? So what if you can reproduce a movie star's face? Or a soup can? That soil in the gallery is a travesty."

"I thought you understood irony," she said. "And context."

"What irony?"

"You have to read the story behind it."

"You shouldn't have to read anything to understand something that should have an immediate impact."

"It had an immediate impact. You're disgusted with it. Some other people might be amused by it. Still others might like the idea. At least it provokes some genuine feeling."

"So does a pile of shit."

She took in a lungful of New York air and gave me an exasperated look. Yellow cabs zoomed by. The sun was beating down on us. Streams of people in T-shirts and shorts walked by. Beggars were perched at almost every corner with their Styrofoam cups.

"Let's get something to drink," I said. "I need some shade."

We found a small diner, around the corner from the Hotel Chelsea on 23rd Street. It was dark and cool inside. We ordered beer and took deep breaths in the draft of the air conditioner.

"Listen to me," she said. "Pay attention."

Her face was set hard, her eyes brilliant in the dim light. I sat back and focused on her.

"We were talking about being unique before," she said.

"Yes."

"And achieving an authentic voice."

"Yes."

"Well, most people are other people, not really themselves at all. They only reproduce other people's thoughts and impressions. Only true artists dare to go deep inside themselves where there's no fakery. Either for pure expressionism or to get rid of all subjectivism, like Cézanne."

"But how many Cézanne's are there? Most of these new so-called artists go deep inside and find nothing but shit."

"True," she said. "But at least they're honest about it. Modern art doesn't cater to the public. It sucks up everything, all the shit included. It challenges. It provokes. It tries to do things in the authentic ways we have forgotten. It takes a stand."

"Yeah," I said, "the *Either* stand."

"Well, what's the *Or* stand?"

"Forget about it," I said.

She stared daggers at me. At moments like this she was magnificent. Her eyes held a strength I admired.

"Only the intense life is worth living, Croach," she said.

"Yeah, but what stays intense for long?"

"I don't know, Croach. You tell me."

In the dim diner her dark eyes shone into me like beacons. I could follow her, they told me. I could surely follow her.

"Croach?" she said.

I couldn't speak. I remembered staring at the northern lights when I was a kid in Northern Ontario. They were sheets of light, green and red and yellow dancing in the void. As if they held the promise of a beauty too far from my reach. And all I could do was stare in awe from the prison of my body.

"Let's go," I said.

As we were getting up from our chairs I impulsively grabbed her and gave her a long kiss. Her lips opened. I tried to suck out her breath. But I only got the stale taste of beer.

The couple at the next table were watching us.

"That's sweet," the middle-aged woman said. She was in a flowery summer dress. Her husband had polyester sansabelt slacks with a camera slung over his shoulder. "Can we take your picture?"

I grabbed Lisa's hand and we hurried out.

Our flight was the next day.

5

From the biographies, from the journals and letters and works, we know that Soren Kierkegaard was born in 1813 and that he died in 1855. That he spent all his life in Copenhagen, in a close-knit society where he knew just about everyone, from king to shopgirl. That he was the youngest of seven children. That his father had made money in the hosiery business. That all but one of Soren's brothers and sisters, along with his mother, died by the time he went to university. That the family thought itself cursed, and that they all suffered extreme melancholy.

We know that S.K. was a spindly guy, with a curved spine that made him stooped, and a mop of unruly fair hair. That he wore glasses, had pale blue eyes, protruding teeth, and receding chin. That, in spite of looking like a gnome, he was a *bon vivant* with his wit and sharp tongue.

We know that he found out about his father's sin, which his father thought accounted for the curse upon the family. That S.K. passed his theological examinations and got engaged to Regine Olsen, but broke the engagement when he realized that he couldn't drag her into his melancholic life. That he remained devoted to her all his life. And left his possessions to her at his death, even though she was long married to someone else.

We know that he wrote half a dozen pseudonymous works, using the Socratic method, presenting us with the stages in life's way to that final "leap." That he openly attacked the established Lutheran Church. That he thought himself a martyr for a Christianity that wasn't practiced any more.

Yet these outward facts about his life can hardly do him justice if not placed against his ideas. For he lived most intensely, as a little-known scholar once wrote about Shakespeare's life, not in the movements of his body, but in the explorations of his mind. That he succeeded in leaving a record of those explorations in the edifice he had built of words.

It was this image that I found appealing about Kierkegaard. And the fact that he tried so desperately to live in that edifice of words. Unlike his adversary, Hegel, who he felt could never live in his.

Since I, too, was seeking to build a house of words, a house not as visible as my father's house, I saw S.K. as my godfather. My daemon to guide me along life's way.

Lisa James, too, lived intensely in her work and in her ideas. That such an attractive and good-hearted girl valued ideas and the artistic life was a rare occurrence in my life's way so far.

After our New York trip later that same summer, we were in her studio in downtown Toronto when she gave me an example of some of her ideas. It was a number of typed sheets she had written for the university. A sort of manifesto of her work.

"I'd like your opinion, Croach," she said. "It goes back to what we were talking about in New York."

The studio was a large room that took up about half of the fifth floor of an old warehouse on Queen, a little removed from the trendy part. She shared it with two other artists, Jonathan Halladay and Evelyn Chu. The south windows were large enough to view the heavens, overlooking the newly made CN Tower and the waterfront.

On a table were the tools of her trade. Used tubes and coffee mugs stained with paint. An assortment of large plastic containers with liquid acrylic paint. Bundles of brushes and palette knives sticking out of tin cans. Broken dishes. Gesso and thinner containers. Air brushes and larger sprays. A chipped bust of some ancient Greek. An old torso. And stacks of magazines.

The floor was heavily stained with drips and sprays of paint. Under the table were two compressors, along with the piles of lumber. In the air was the smell of paint thinners, linseed oil, and oxides.

On the wall behind the table she had tacked old photographs, pictures, and personal tokens. A short strand of birch bark. A large feather. A fragment of stained glass. Various postcards of famous artworks. And photos of abandoned industrial sites and the husks of ugly machinery.

On the wall in her corner area were various prints of the people who had influenced her work. Examples of geometric forms without any representation. Tension in lines and colours alone. One edge hitting another. A print by her old teacher, Guido Molinari. A Yves Gaucher, another Quebec artist she admired. And a Josef Albers. She also had an example of Emily Carr's work, a large totem. And my favourite, a Lawren Harris. The Harris painting had a large tree stump set high on a rocky shore thrusting into the sky. On the upper left hand corner sharp bands of golden light flooded clouds that looked more like Michelin tires. Its simple intensity sacrificed all exactitude.

"Harris is the only Group of Seven painter I like," Lisa had told me. "He was into Eastern religion and spirituality. He was a great lover of nature. He felt you had to live in it and experience it before you could dare to depict it.

48

First he was into the faithful recreation of nature. Then he tried to simplify and intensify everything. Simplicity and intensity, Croach. That's what we should strive for."

Apparently Harris, along with other Group of Seven artists, had lived in my neck of the woods, north of Sault Ste. Marie, in the Agawa Canyon area.

A few large canvases from her recent series of hard-edge paintings were lined up against the wall. Today she was photographing them for her portfolio to take around to the various galleries to drum up interest for exhibits. Her Nikon was on a tripod.

It was an overcast muggy day outside. A reflector and a lamp with a large umbrella-like filter were lighting the canvases.

I sat on a heavily stained sofa close to the table, reading what she entitled her Statement of Rationale.

"Remember what you told me about Virginia Woolf at the New York Public Library?" she said. "I've used some of that. You can keep that. I have another copy."

As she was leaning over to peer into the camera, I noticed how her overlarge plaid work shirt rode up her butt. Every so often as I read I looked up to observe her.

My first series of paintings and drawings is called the Consciousness Series. It consists of fourteen acrylic/airbrush paintings, seven of which are 6'-8' and seven 3'-5'. Along with seven pencil drawings.

Consciousness is derived from two Latin words: com: together, and scire: to know. So that conscire alii, for the Romans, meant to know with another (or common awareness) and conscire sibi meant what one knows individually (unique awareness).

For humans, the predominant form of consciousness is

vision. With vision we comprehend. We understand. Vision is light.

In my Consciousness Series black is total unconsciousness. Pre-life. Death. Nothingness. Void. But from this void and death comes nascent light in different intervals, intensities, and distances in space. The void dominates physical space, but the light edges in sharply to be seen by a viewer with an aperture that is open to the cosmos.

I looked at her. "*Pardonnez-moi?*"

She set up another canvas. As she moved I noticed the tight crease at her crotch. She held her head high as she pursed her lips and explained.

"Don't pretend to be so dense, Croach. I'm trying to understand how we get perspective. Insight. Awareness. I think it's just a struggle between light and dark. Chemical reactions. One hundred billion neurons that fire electrical impulses through their tendrils into gaps called synapses."

I read on, shaking my head.

An area of canvas is a rectangle of flat, blank space. Through successive coats of gesso and sanding an immaculate surface is prepared. This mechanistic process reflects the culture in which we live. For me, this action, in which I use my hands in a series of repetitions, becomes a ritual. My hands come into contact with each inch of the surface of the canvas. I have to feel the canvas. I have to touch and smell it.

My whole body has to be a part of the creation. All that is applied onto the canvas – the paint, the gesso, the water – is pumped through the compressor of the heart.

I looked up to her canvases against the wall. They were

predominantly black, with light in various tones and intensities, creating whorls and lines of hard-edge and soft glows. They looked like solar eclipses, sheets of light like the borealis except uncoloured, all against the darkest dark of endless space. Since the black had been applied by airbrush, layer upon layer, it had an eerie depth to it, as if it could swallow up the viewer if he got too close.

Though she dressed in black and earth tones and never wore colourful clothing, Lisa wasn't a dark and gloomy person. She was usually cheerful and playful, smiling in that gleeful toothy way that escalated into a chuckle of amusement if I said anything remotely funny.

"So?" I said. "I still don't get it."

"It's all very scientific, Croach," she went back to photographing her work. "There's no ghost in the machine. No soul that survives our body's death. All these myths and illusions we have, they can all be explained. They can be reduced to chemical reactions that produce energy. That's what my father used to tell me. He used to set up his telescope in the back verandah with the skylight. I used to look at the heavens and stars and planets and be mesmerized. All that darkness and the twinkling light. Then he'd tell me about the advent of life. From gases like nitrogen, carbon dioxide, ammonia, methane. And the heat from the sun. And water vapour too. Over billions of years. You'd get molecular chains, like amino acids, proteins, and DNA – the blueprint of life. And from single-celled life-forms, you got more complicated life-forms that needed to reconnect in order to reproduce."

"You mean sex?"

"Yes."

"Christ, it sounds so simple," I said. "Everything reduced to chemical reactions – and chance, of course.

What about free will? And Reason? And our ability to laugh and lie?"

"Those are highly developed neural reactions."

"So your art is simply a highly developed neural reaction?"

"Yes," she laughed.

"What about the darkness?"

"What about it?"

"Was it always there?"

"The darkness is the void. Nothingness. Light is energy. Heat. Matter. The light can't be seen in the void unless it hits another piece of matter."

"But what comes first, darkness or light? Being or nothingness?"

"I don't know. They co-exist."

"Okay, then. You be the darkness and I'll be the light. We'll bang into each other. Hard."

"I don't know."

"Come here," I said.

"I'm busy, Croach."

"Come here. Let's connect in the cosmic dance. Let me take a leap into the darkness."

She lay down on the sofa with me.

"You know what I like about you," I told her. "You get so sexy when you talk ideas."

"Shut up," she laughed. "I was serious. In the end all we have, Croach, is the light and the dark."

When I was inside her, feeling her body grip me with the energy of the earth, I tried to keep hold of myself. To prolong the intensity. I thought of another struggle between the light and the dark. Plato's cave. Of the guy who breaks free of the shackles, Socrates says. Who is so used to seeing the shadows on the cave wall that when he goes out into the natural light of the sun he's blinded. I

52

imagined I was that guy. I was blinded by the sun. And that when I went back to report my discovery no one believed me. Like Cassandra.

I could only think like this for a while.

Lisa gripped me hard. Her power was more than a match for mine.

Soon my mind turned to a delicious mush and I felt myself being pulled into the hot bowels of the earth.

6

For the summer we had sublet a flat in a large Victorian house in the Annex north of the university. One of Lisa's painter friends had gone off to Europe and given us the place dirt cheap. All we had to do was water her plants.

About two blocks away was the rooming house where I had hit rock bottom after dropping out of the graduate programme. In that time, before the Italian trip, I had almost totally disconnected myself from family and friends, thinking that the solitude would gain me some sort of heroic perspective. I used to read my godfathers and godmothers with such hungry eyes it was like sucking up their black blood through a straw.

The Annex had changed since those days. The Victorian houses – all as large as Spanish galleons, with turrets and porches and foyers – had been sandblasted and renovated, made into chic offices for lawyers and charitable organizations. Where once I had seen flags and bed sheets as curtains and dog shit on the front grass, I now saw expensive office equipment and brass nameplates.

I was beginning to see how impermanent everything was. People were concentrating on making money now. A new era had begun.

I wore cut-off jeans and a T-shirt. I rode my battered ten-speed everywhere and kept it chained outside in the cool narrow alleyway where a cement runnel carried the water to the street.

The summer was hot and muggy. The heavy air gained

weight under a hazy sun only visible through the constant smog. The heat sucked all our energy and body fluids. I cycled like a madman and played tennis at the Trinity College courts under the blazing sun. It didn't take long before I became bone thin. My skin tanned easily and deeply. My hair was long and thick, parted in the middle. Lisa constantly flattered my looks, called me a blue-eyed Italian. She wanted to photograph me, or paint a portrait.

"Can you actually paint a recognizable person?" I asked her.

"Just because I do hard-edge and abstract it doesn't mean I can't do representational stuff. You look quite gorgeous. I can make an exception for you."

The flattery went straight to my head. I didn't have much of a chance to be vain in the past. Now women noticed me a little longer. Perfect strangers came up to me to say hello. I felt giddy with self-confidence. For so many years, with my face splotched with acne, with my desperate shyness and self-imposed aloofness, I had been invisible.

Fortunately Lisa's parents had given us an air conditioner. Otherwise it would've been unbearable in the third-floor flat. We kept it in the den, in a window overlooking the street. The den was my work area. On the antique roll-top desk I had my ink bottle, fountain pens, and exercise notebooks. Potted plants surrounded the desk. The panelled walls had framed posters of art exhibits from the Prado, the Uffizi, and the Tate. Beside the reading chair, an old rocker with an ancient cushion seat, was a pile of books.

I had bought postcards of David's *The Death of Socrates* and Lawren Harris's *North Shore, Lake Superior* and pinned them on the wall over my desk.

Every morning I worked at the roll-top desk – still the

same novel about immigrant Italians. This was when I lived most intensely. In silence. Not in the movements of my body. But in the subterranean passages of dream and myth, where the black blood flowed more easily, crossing from the darkness into the light, from the invisible to the visible. Here I could build my edifice of words. My house of being.

Lisa got up later. Most times she took the bus to her studio. In the afternoons I had my Shakespeare course at Victoria College. Then I'd change in the basement wash-rooms and cycle over to the St. Hilda's residence, to the Trinity courts.

That summer I felt myself smiling all the time, greeting strangers in a buoyant jocular mood. It was mostly from being with Lisa, I knew. Basking in the glow of her body. Her laughter. Her fine spirit. Her sense of play. She made me happy. She helped to restore my self-confidence. These were feelings I hadn't experienced since my childhood in the West End.

My sickness of soul I kept to myself. Locked away in a compartment that was close to being like the Bull of Pharsalis that S.K. talked about. Suffering was necessary for the poet, S.K. said. But it should come out as music to the ears.

I had a picture of my daemon, that thin rake of a Dane, in my mind all the time. Understand life backwards, but live it forwards, he kept telling me. When you get to the Great Paradox, he said, get ready to make your leap.

Would I have the guts to make that leap?

One evening after making love on the floor beside the coffee table where we had just eaten our meal, I teased Lisa about doing a portrait of me.

"I don't believe you can draw a likeness," I said.

She had made a delicious omelet, her favourite dish. They came out of the oven large and fluffy, overflowing with vegetables, cheese, and whatever else she could find. The wine and food made her amorous. She stepped over the coffee table and pounced on me before I could finish my food. "I'm going to eat you all up," she said, laughing.

"You're getting to be all bones," she said, her cheek on my chest. "I'd have to draw a likeness of a skeleton pretty soon."

"Come on," I flexed my biceps. "Look at this."

"You're so vain," she laughed. "If I painted you it might turn out to be another Albright."

"What?"

"He painted Dorian Gray."

"Why aren't you vain?" I asked her.

"Oh, I'm vain."

"I don't think so. You deliberately hide your figure. You never wear skirts. And no makeup or perfume."

"I don't want any trouble with men. When I was a teenager my worst fear was of getting raped. It's still my worst fear. You men never have that fear."

"We have other fears."

"Such as?"

"Such as not being able to satisfy a woman."

"Love satisfies a woman. Sex is just part of that love. Besides, that's not a fear. It's more an anxiety."

I paused, not wanting to enter that territory straight on. Her body purred as I stroked her hair. I trailed my fingers over her high forehead and the taut skin around her eyes. I felt the shape of her skull.

"Anxiety?" I said.

"When a man has sex, he's basically having sex with himself. Trying to live up to his own expectations. When

57

a woman has sex, she's basically trying to please the man. Men are so wrapped up in themselves. And women are taught early on to be an appendage of men. It's all that Adam and Eve crap."

"Tell me what I can do to please you more."

"If I have to tell you, Croach, you'll never know. It's not knowing. It's doing it from the heart. Doing it because you can't stop yourself."

I raised my eyebrows, as if she had reprimanded me.

She laughed. "Don't worry, Croach," she said in a soft voice. "Just be yourself. I like you the way you are, believe me. Except I'd like you to go down on me too every so often."

That week I called Gene Marinelli. He arranged a meeting with us at a posh French restaurant across from Yorkville. He had a former student he wanted us to meet. "A looker with a good mind," he said. "But she'll have to stack up against Lisa if she's going to pass the test."

He liked Lisa very much. It was the only thing he envied about me. He was close to his doctorate. I was a mere high-school teacher and had no books published. Lisa, stunning and bright, mothered him and flattered his intellectual pretensions. She knew just how to handle him.

Gene was desperate to find a job at a respectable university, and not out in the boonies. He had been a lecturer at the Erindale campus the past two years. His contract was up. He was also anxious to start a normal life, with a smart woman and a family.

"I haven't been out on a regular date for so long," he told me. "I forget what to do."

Women found him either intimidating or overly meek. From the outside he gave the impression of a thin and wiry academic. Coal black short hair. Thick-rim glasses.

Heavy shadow of a beard. On the inside he had developed the iron will and the pretensions to greatness that had been inspired in him by Allan Bloom, his doctoral supervisor.

"I want Lisa to have a look at her," he told me on the phone. "She has good judgment on these matters. You've got close to the perfect girl there, Trecroci. I'd marry her immediately if I were you. What're you waiting for?"

"Good question."

"This is Victoria Downes," he introduced his friend in the foyer of the restaurant. It was a renovated house with a canopy over the doorway.

She was very blond, light-skinned, tall and willowy – quite his opposite. Lisa gave me a knowing look.

She had this theory about Gene. She admired his scholarly determination, tolerated his affectations like the beret and cigars and navy topcoats copied from Bloom, even put up with his conservative political views, but she thought it was all an expertly contrived ruse.

"Underneath he's a child in the real world," she told me. "He's lived so much in the airy field of abstract thought he's kept his sensuality bottled up. As soon as he gets his job, he's going to break out. Believe me."

Inside it was dim and pretentious, with waiters decked in penguin suits and small aprons, looking like they had stepped right off a *bateau* on the Seine.

Victoria was quiet as we made our orders. She was in a stylish pastel pant-suit. It made her look like candy floss. Her blue eyes, however, were alert to us. Lisa was in casual dress slacks and an olive green silk top, with no frills, affecting a casual elegance. Her long neck was bare. Her hair was piled up.

Gene tried to get Victoria to open up to us as we sipped

our wine. We learned she was in law school and her father was a lawyer. He did corporate work for a prestigious firm downtown.

"One has to be quite confident and eloquent, maybe even a little arrogant, to be a lawyer, wouldn't you say?" Gene looked at Lisa. "The knock against women is that they're not tough enough in the business and practical worlds where lives and money are at stake."

"I'd never last a week in that world," Lisa stated. "Not that I'm not tough enough. I just wouldn't take it seriously. All those deceptive fronts and posturings. Everyone looking after their own interests. I'd be too considerate of my adversaries. In court, for example, I'd probably knit my opponent a sweater."

Gene laughed, fawning over her words. I could see he was trying to get a rise out of Victoria.

"Women can be just as tough," Victoria said in a challenging tone, "and not lose any feminine appeal either. The problem's not with women – but with the way men perceive them."

"What do you think, Mark?" Gene tried to get me into the fray.

"*Esse est percipi*," I said.

Victoria gave me a cursory glance, waited for a translation, then completely disregarded me.

"There are some cultures," she said, "where women do all the heavy work and the men simply preen and take lice out of their hair before going off to hunt and do battle."

"The eye sees, but the mind perceives," Lisa said, looking at me and disregarding Victoria.

"Now, now," Gene raised his hand, as if to give absolution. "We're talking at cross purposes. If you're female, it doesn't necessarily mean you're a woman."

We were talking with a straight face. Victoria looked at us, bewildered.

"Are you making fun of me?" she said.

"Of course not," Gene said.

"I admit I feel a little intimidated. But only because I'm outnumbered."

"According to Socrates, intimidation is the beginning of true knowledge," I came in, feeling some sympathy for her.

"Outnumbered by whom?" Gene said.

"By artist-types," she said.

"Look, guys," he raised his hand again like a baton, "stop being artist-types. And be a little civil towards our guest."

A few days later I heard Lisa talking to Gene on the phone.

"She's not your type," Lisa said. "I'd go for someone without any brains but has a good heart. Someone who will take care of you. That's what you need, Gene. As soon as Victoria gets over her admiration for you as her former teacher, she'll put you on trial for living too much in your mind."

7

Anxiety.

S.K. had a lot to say about anxiety. And despair. And dread. Emotions, all of them. The inner state of the soul. Some scholars called him a psychologist, and not a philosopher at all. How small their outlook! How paltry their metaphysics!

I was trying to understand my daemon backwards and, of course, trying to live life forwards.

After Shakespeare class one Monday evening the teacher, Jill Corbenson, invited us to her place for wine and cheese. It was on the other side of Queen's Park from Victoria College, on a sidestreet off Spadina.

Angela DiGiorgi, an attractive teacher in her mid-thirties from North York, offered to drive me there. My bike was locked outside of the Vic building. Angela had her light brown hair in 1940s fashion and wore colourful summer dresses. She stared at me with Ingrid Bergman eyes. The ones that said, Play it, Sam. Her lips had that puffy kissable allure to them.

"We'll always have Paris," I said to her one time.

"What?"

"Here's looking at you, kid."

She looked cool in the wilting summer evenings and smelled of exotic perfumes. I'd talk to her during breaks in the Vic basement lounge where we had vending machines and carried on conversations over Shakespearean psychology. Jill Corbenson, taught by Alfred Harbage

"Life's too dull without poetry," he told us. "I welcome more women in the arts."

Corbenson told us she had Paul as a student before. His writing was atrocious, but he got great marks for livening up the class and for "dedication" to the Bard.

"I don't get it," an older Scots woman, Pam Nettleton, said beside him. "Six times! Why?"

She wore too much makeup. Her silvery hair was permed. Her thin face bore some resemblance to Virginia Woolf.

"Why do we do anything?" he said and paused with just the right timing. "For love." Then he looked so deeply into Pam's eyes that she lowered her face.

Jill Corbenson laughed. "Paul's a genuine lover . . . of Shakespeare. He doesn't care about his marks. And he's not out to show the teacher up."

I sat on a metal lawn chair, on my fifth or sixth glass of wine. My bare legs in shorts were glued to the paint. I inhaled Angela's perfume. Whenever a skeeter got whacked by the hot plate I winced.

I looked up at the sky and saw a full moon. I felt light-headed and careless.

"Passion is the real thing," I barked out. "The real measure of our power. And the age in which we live is wretched because it's without passion."

They all turned their heads towards me.

"Which play is that from?" Paul said.

"That my lover-friend is the melancholic Dane."

"I don't remember that line from *Hamlet*."

I stared at him.

They stared back at me, waiting for more.

"He means Kierkegaard," Corbenson said, pursing her lips in feigned amusement.

"That's right. You're so right. Kudos to you, Ms. Corbenson."

A few of the ladies giggled. Angela put her hand on my arm, as if to stop me from crashing into a non-existent windshield.

Corbenson gave me a wary look and stayed quiet.

"Give me that man that is not passion's slave," Paul intoned, "and I will wear him in my heart's core."

"Oh, to have passion for the divine," I rambled on, unable to restrain myself, making a fool of myself. "How many of you will come to the Archimedean Point? How many? What we need now is not rational people but martyrs who will run headlong against the human discovery, progress."

I knew I was drunk. I couldn't help myself. I was usually quiet and shy in gatherings like this. Corbenson was starting to look worried. Angela beside me was the librarian-damsel I had to fight for.

"You're not making any sense, Mr. Trecroci," Corbenson said.

Angela led me to the car a little later.

"Where's my bike?" I said, teetering slightly.

"I'll drive you home," she said. "You're in no condition to ride a bike at night."

Inside the car I leaned my head back as Angela drove towards the Annex. I gave her directions. She parked on the street under the trees at the corner away from our house.

"Is this it?" she peered out, at no particular house.

It was all dark, the tall elm and oak trees obscuring most of the street lamps.

We made a lot of small talk. She told me about her sad life. She had been close to marriage twice. Once the guy turned out to be gay. She thought she was doomed.

"That's good," I said. "Very good. The door is open for wisdom."

"Are you with someone, Mark?" she asked me. As she moved ever so slightly in the driver's seat, I could sense the friction of undergarments against flesh. I could smell the scent of perfume.

"Yes," I said.

But in getting out of the car, I made a slight hesitation, leaned forward as if to whisper goodbye and we suddenly were clutching at each other.

She drew away from me and took long breaths.

"D'you know that Paul guy?" she said, showering me with words and perfume. "He's not really a Shakespeare nut. He takes all those courses to meet women. D'you know he's made a pass at every woman in the course, except for Pam. She's next on his list."

I was on her again. She had such kissable lips, even though she was too much of a talker. I worked on her lips, probed them, mashed them, licked them, then stuck my tongue deep inside her mouth, and her body went limp on me.

I said stupid things to her, tracing her lips with my finger.

Her eyes were closed, her lips partly opened. My left arm was around her neck cradling her head, my right finger traced a path down her throat, between her breasts, over her stomach. Her body was quivering.

I stopped. Restrained myself. I could feel the elastic of her underpants, the warm skin underneath her dress. But I pulled back.

"What's the matter?" she said, sitting upright.

"Either I stay . . . or I go."

"All right," she said, angry. "Go if you must."

The moment passed. She looked at me. We were strangers again. I turned the door handle.

"Will I see you in class?" she said.

"Of course."

"How old are you?"

When I told her she shook her head.

Later, as I was walking up the stairs of the house, guilt assailed me. I wiped my mouth. Her saliva was still on me. In my mouth. In my head.

Fortunately Lisa was at her studio, working late at night to complete some work for an upcoming exhibition. I had time to adjust, to wash away the perfume that lingered over my body like fallout.

Let's face it, S.K. said in my ear, it's Lisa's love for you that makes you desirable to other women.

You're a very powerful guy, he added, but your power is not that of a ruler or conqueror, for the only power you have is the power to hold yourself in check.

After my shower I made a little snack. Cheese. Bread. Fruit. And watched TV, waiting for Lisa to come home. Would she know? I asked myself, as I watched the helpless figures on the screen, who were unable to hold themselves in check, indulging in their every desire.

I suddenly remembered my bike locked at the Vic fence. It would be there all night. Anyone could come along and steal it.

8

Lisa and her two associates were having a little party in the studio to celebrate their new exhibition at a gallery around the corner from the Discount King, Honest Ed's. We had spent the day moving canvases and sculptures with a rent-a-truck. It wasn't easy work. Lisa had her huge canvases. Jon Halladay had large bronze sculptures of hands and fingers that weighed a ton.

Evelyn Chu's theme was the vulva. She painted it in every conceivable colour and perspective and size. Her titles told the story. *The Birth of the World. Beaver Trap,* which was a mouse trap inside the gaping hole. *Holiday Surprise. Vag Itation.* Lisa and I had fun with these titles. Not within earshot of Evelyn, though, who was a dead-serious lesbian and a committed feminist. She wanted to create an energy field around the vulva. Give it back its rightful power taken away by such bastards as Sigmund Freud and Friedrich Nietzsche.

She had a fuck-the-past attitude.

And looked like a choir boy. In her late twenties, she had close-cropped hair and a stringy body. She dressed in ripped denims and T-shirts, with a cigarette dangling from her lips. Very Jimmy Dean-ish. Lisa told me, however, that it was just a pose. Underneath, Evelyn was very feminine. She was going through a phase. Every artist went through a phase.

"Her parents have disowned her," Lisa told me. "So she's gone off the deep end to make a statement."

I was talking to Jon Halladay and his girlfriend, Isabella Nardi, off in the corner close to the sofa and fridge. Evelyn came over to thank me for helping them out.

"We needed your muscle," she told me, smiling at Bella.

Bella was the only woman in a dress. A striking blue outfit that made her stand out amongst the denim and shirts. She was thin and attractive, with tweezer legs and sharp features. Large soft eyes that looked at you as you wanted to be seen.

"What about my muscle?" Jon said in a straight face.

"Your muscle's wasted, man."

"Not on you," he smiled.

Jon was a broad-shouldered good-looking guy with blond spiked hair and a goatee. He had slow movements. Spoke slow. Walked slow. Nothing fazed him. He drank vodka out of a tall glass with ice.

There were a number other people I didn't recognize. Friends of Evelyn and Jon's. One was obviously another butch girl. She was talking to Lisa on the other side of the studio.

Lisa knew Jon and Evelyn from her student days at Concordia. They got along. But they varied greatly in their artwork and philosophies.

"Thanks anyway," Evelyn said to me. "How's your work going?"

I told them about the book I was working on. A homage to my father who had worked in the steel plant for twenty years.

"The only image of the Italian male out there," I told them, "is that of the mobster, the mafia-hoodlum. The gangster hero. Someone who goes to church one day and whacks someone the next. What about the hard-working immigrant? What about the dependable hard-hat who really cares for his family? Is he ever made into a hero? No! He's entirely invisible."

"Yeah!" Evelyn raised her fist. "Everything's image. Surface image. Even if you rip away surface layer, you have another layer of image. What are you if not your fucken layers of image? There's nothing in the middle. Why d'you think my parents had a spaz when I told them I was gay? They were concerned about their image in the Chinese community. They weren't concerned about me, that's for fucken sure. You think I'm paying homage to them?"

"Cool it, Ev," Jon said.

"You cool it," she looked at him.

"Ah, Ev," Jon said. "You can't expect them to chuck thousands of years of culture for your benefit. You expect too much from them."

"Don't give me that shit. Parents are supposed to love you unconditionally."

"What I've found," I ventured carefully, "is that if you've gone beyond your parents in insight, wisdom, what have you, the onus is on you to be accommodating."

"Pardon me?" she craned her neck towards me. "What makes you the authority on my life?"

"I'm just stating an opinion."

"I never had any trouble with my parents," Bella said.

"That's easy for you to say, babe," Evelyn narrowed her eyes at her.

"I'm just saying I envy you your problems. Maybe that's how you get to be an artist."

"Good. Very good," I nodded. "That's quite an insightful remark. The theory is, the artist has a wound that can't be healed unless the pure knight of art comes and redeems him."

"That's shit too!" Evelyn waved her hand at me.

"Made by male legend-mongers. Those who have any talent, on the other hand, just do it. And generally don't know why."

"Don't kid yourself," Jon said to her. "You have a vision like everyone else. Or you wouldn't paint those snatches all the time."

"Shut up with that word, I told you."

They stared at each other, and let it pass.

I couldn't resist. "I'm sure it's occurred to you guys. I mean, one of you does only hands and fingers. And the other does vaginas."

"Yeah, so?" Evelyn said.

"So, add one and one."

"What're you trying to say?" Evelyn raised her hands, her feet set apart.

Lisa came over. "What're you guys shouting about? I can hear you across the room."

"Your boyfriend here," Evelyn said, "is trying to be funny."

"I'm not her *boyfriend*."

"What the fuck are you, then?"

"I object to that word."

Her veins were popping out of her neck. "Give me another one."

"I'm a midwife in the boulevard of barren wombs."

Evelyn Chu took a step towards me. "Are you trying to be funny?"

"Hey, if you can't laugh at yourself, others will laugh at you."

"Fuck off!" she snarled, and marched away to be with her girlfriend.

Lisa shook her head at me. "You have a way of alienating people quickly."

"Call me Socrates Unbound."

Later the portable stereo on the paint table was blaring away. I had drunk a few beers and was feeling light-headed. I sat with Bella Nardi on the sofa. Where Lisa and I had made love a few times. The stuffing was oozing out.

A few couples were dancing in the open area beyond Jon's artspace. Among them were Lisa and Jon. Evelyn and her friend, Alice.

"So," I said casually to Bella, "you seem like a well-adjusted person who's never had any major problems."

"I guess I'm too ordinary," she shrugged.

"Nothing wrong with that."

"I'm glad you think so. It depends on how you look at it, I guess."

"Right," I stared at the dancers, "it all depends on perspective."

I heard my daemon's voice inside my left ear. From the chapter called The Diary of a Seducer. He told me to desire nothing that wasn't freely given. He told me the highest enjoyment was in being loved.

"Have you and Jon been together long?" I said, my eyes lingering on the dancers.

"Six months or so," Bella said. "What about you and Lisa?"

"Oh, it's been years now. But on and off, really. I don't live here, you know." I mentioned my hometown up north.

"Yeah, Jon told me," she said. "I've got an aunt and uncle up there, you know. It's a small world, isn't it?"

The music stopped and the dancers came back to us, all flushed and chatty.

The smell of paint and thinners rose from the sofa into my nostrils.

The odours brought to mind our house under the bridge. My father's masterpiece. There wasn't a day when he wasn't working on it. He had bought it for a pittance in the late 1950s. It was a two-storey wood-frame without a basement in the crossfire of the three major industries of the city. I remembered it looking more like an overgrown shack. The original siding was begrimed by decades of smoke from the pulp mill, the chrome plant, and the steel plant.

"The Italians in this neighbourhood," my father told me, "we fix up our houses, that's only the one thing."

But while we were hammering in all those nails and painting and repainting, the International Bridge was being built right over our heads, devaluing the house we were so diligently upgrading.

Sometimes I could look at these artists with the eyes of my father. They'd seem totally impractical. They seemed at once naive and self-indulgent.

I could picture my father coming home from his shift at the steel plant every day and putting on his green work pants and plaid shirt. He never stopped working. His hands were never idle.

Later Jon drove us home in the rent-a-truck.

"Ev can be a bitch," he said to me. "You have to take her with a grain of salt."

"It's just a pose," Lisa said, sitting between us.

"Eventually the pose becomes the person," Jon said.

In bed, before we shut off the lights, Lisa cuddled up to me.

"I can't have children, Croach," she said. "I'm so afraid. If I ever had kids it would be the end of my painting. I know it. I couldn't do both jobs. I just couldn't. I'd devote my whole life to the kids, I know it. Believe me,

Croach. I have to choose. I don't want to be a mediocre artist. Painting is my life. You understand. I know you do."

9

Towards the end of the summer Lisa got more affectionate as my time to depart drew nearer. She kept me in bed until ten or eleven when I should've been working. She cuddled up to me on the sofa after supper as I read.

One evening she took the book I was reading away from me and gave me a long serious look.

"Let's go to Paris next summer," she said.

"Sure. That sounds good."

After a pause, she said, "I'll come up to visit you, okay?"

"Sure."

"Meet your parents."

"Okay."

"I'm serious."

I looked into her eyes to see what she was getting at. I tried to see past the opening of the sockets. Down the nerves and into the cavern to the actual wall itself.

"I'm beginning to miss you already," she said.

I snuggled up to her and took her in my arms. We talked for another hour. It was too much talk. I was exhausted afterwards. I couldn't hear myself think. I felt honoured, like one entrusted with a great pearl, but she took up so much of my time.

The next day I met Angela at the Robarts Library and we went across the street to the Eatery at Innis College. It was very bright inside, with plenty of windows and potted plants. Angela was in a yellow drop-waist dress and matching handbag. Her hair swished as she moved. Her smile was radiant.

She was like a confection in comparison to Lisa. It made the illicit rendez-vous all the more exciting. I was playing at having lunch. I was playing at the easy charm. I was playing at my cool indifference to her dalliance with me. Indifference and detachment gave everything an air of make-believe.

I had gone through high school and university without knowing women, and so desperately aching for them. It was as if every woman and girl who had ignored me had hurt me.

Angela glowed whenever I complimented her.

"You look so good," I said under the overarching plants.

We sat at the glass wall overlooking the fortress-like library across the street. The sun felt good on my skin. The air conditioner kept us cool. We were in a manufactured paradise. I was the Adam. She was the apple.

We talked nonsense and drank wine.

She wasn't looking forward to going back to teaching. She wanted to spend a whole year in France. Her two cats were moulting too much.

It doesn't matter what she's saying, Johannes the Seducer told me. She's a ripe delicious apple. All rosy and bursting with energy. But the apple doesn't want to be plucked. It wants to be admired, coddled, polished to a gleaming brightness. And then it'll drop on its own.

Before Lisa, he said, you were too sexually desperate. You approached women from a position of need. A position of weakness. Now, sexually sated, you can look past your needs and into the heart of each woman's needs. You can look into the places she needs to be admired. Where she needs the intimacy. Where she needs the danger or the amusement.

"I'll walk you to your car," I suggested after the meal. For some reason it was parked on the other side of the campus, at the St. Mike's lot.

We strolled across Queen's Park. It was a hazy summer day. With warm moist air coming up to my nostrils. The smell of the leaves and grass was strong. Every so often her perfume penetrated me. Swirled in my head.

I took her hand. I stayed quiet in order to bask in the warmth of the day and to experience her presence. They were enough. They felt so good. A pretty woman. A beautiful day. I was swimming in warm colours, scents, images. Nothing could be more simple or intense than that.

Under a tree, close to the equestrian statue in the middle of the park, she stopped me and held my gaze.

"I don't know what's happening," she said.

"Nothing's happening," I said.

I searched her eyes. Looked deeply into them. Past the colour of her pupils. Past her age and sexual allure. To see who she was.

Whatever you do, Johannes told me, don't touch her. Don't break the spell. The illusion of the moment.

She dropped her gaze.

"What're you doing?" she said.

"I'm just feeling so good," I said. "The day. You with me. I feel fantastic. I'm capable of doing anything today."

"I don't understand," she said, not looking at me, "you're going away soon. You're involved with another woman. And you're so much younger than me. I'm such a fool."

"Why?" I squeezed her hand. "You're thinking of the past. You're thinking of the future. You're losing the moment."

She looked at me for a long time.

"Look," I said. "Forget about it, okay. I'll walk you to the car."

We walked hurriedly to the parking lot. Traffic swirled around the oval park. The air between us was tense. The afternoon sun was too hot. I felt sticky with perspiration under my tight jeans. I should've worn shorts. I shouldn't have drunk so much wine.

At her car in front of the gothic St. Basil's church I gave her a hard look.

"Goodbye. See you next year."

"Wait a minute," she said as I turned to walk away. "I'll give you a lift home."

"It's okay. I'd rather walk."

"Please, Mark. I don't want it to end like this. I'll give you a lift home."

I got in without further word. She drove silently up Bay through the mid-afternoon traffic. The car smelled new. Her scent, mixed with the newness of the upholstery, swirled up into my nostrils. I could feel the wine in my head, diluting the past, killing the future. I felt invincible. Alive with energy.

When she stopped in front of the house, I said thanks, it's been good knowing you. Give me a ring if you're ever up north in the land that time forgot.

But she kept me in the car and finally broke down. She was sorry, she said, if she was rude. But I scared her. She didn't know what to make of me. She just didn't want to let me go, but how did she know she could trust me?

She took out a handkerchief. Her face became wet. I sat still. Whatever you do, Johannes said, don't touch her.

"It's all right," I said. "No harm done. It was good. We

don't really know each other. Forget about trust. Let's just say goodbye and leave it at that."

"No, no," she sobbed. "Not yet. Is she up there?"

"No, she's at her studio."

I didn't budge. I could easily have gotten out of the car. I had the power to resist. To hold back. To let things happen as they happened. I was no longer desperate. I had the power of indifference.

"Please, Mark," Angela said, leaning towards me. She put her flower-scented head on my shoulder. "I'm a fool, but let's go up."

"Are you sure?"

"Yes."

We went up the stairs together, but it was she leading the dance. It was awkward for a while in the apartment. Angela looked around, needed time to adjust, then threw herself in my arms. And it was she who hungrily kissed me. Led me to the bedroom. So that I forgot for long stretches of time it was Lisa's bed we were on.

Angela let herself go. She was silly putty. Her skin was bleached white. It was alive to every touch and caress. If I even went near her stomach she quivered.

Then I became curiously detached. There and not there. Separated from my own pleasure. She seemed a doll under me. She was inside her desperate needs. It gave me pleasure to ease her up to where she needed to go.

Afterwards we lay in bed in tense silence. As if we had committed a crime.

"It's terrible, terrible," she muttered, facing away from me. "I've never done anything like this before."

I stayed quiet.

"You can't love her," Angela said.

I stared at her.

"When's she coming back? Tell me. I won't be able to face myself tomorrow. I'm so shameless. How old are you again?"

The more she talked, the smaller she became in my eyes. When she was caught in her passion she was a tigress of hunger. She was a goddess of need. Now she was reverting to her ordinary self. Small-minded. Petty.

"Angela, be quiet," I shushed her.

"How can I be quiet?" she got upset. "This whole room smells of her. Don't you think I can smell her here? I feel like an invader. I've invaded her space. I've trespassed on her domain."

"Don't be ridiculous. This isn't really her room. We've sublet the flat."

"You don't know what I'm talking about. Men are so blind. She's here, I tell you. Those are her things on the vanity dresser. Those are her clothes I see inside the closet. These are the sheets she's laundered."

She sounded like a person I didn't know again.

"Stop it!" I raised my voice.

All the good feelings and illusions of our love-making had disappeared.

That's the problem with the aesthetic stage, Kierkegaard told me. Nothing is maintained. Everything is passing, transitory. The moment is lost.

After a moment Angela settled down. She cuddled up to me. Put her head on my chest. Made cooing sounds. "I'm sorry, Mark. But I shouldn't have come here."

"I'm the one taking the big risk." Now I sounded petty.

A little later I told Angela she had to go. It didn't take her long to collect her things and freshen up in the bathroom.

"Call me tomorrow," she gave me a last kiss before hurrying down the stairs.

Interestingly enough, seeing her going down those stairs tugged at my heart moreso than all the time she was in the flat. She seemed vulnerable, endearing, an attractive older woman trying to make do with a hopeless relationship.

It was four o'clock. Lisa would be back in an hour or so.

I rushed to the bedroom and quickly changed the sheets and made the bed. In the bathroom I scoured the sink for loose hair and did some wiping up before I took a long shower. Afterwards I closed all the windows and turned the air conditioner full blast. Soon the flat was cold enough to freeze any lingering smells.

This is what you've become, I said to my reflection in the kitchen mirror. A petty two-timer. A schemer. A sheet-changer. A liar and deceiver. A manipulator of women.

I smiled at the reflection. The blue eyes stared back in icy relief. The hair was long and thick. The torso was lean. I couldn't help feeling good. I was no longer a victim of women. No longer a victim of my body's hunger for women. I had turned the tables. I felt at home in my body. What more could a man want?

As I diced the vegetables for one of Lisa's omelets, I wondered if she would sense that something had changed in me. I wondered if she'd know that another woman had been here.

But so what if she did? I thought. Women couldn't hurt me. They couldn't control me. I was the one to hurt them.

You're such a fool, S.K. whispered in my ear.

10

In 1835 S.K. was halfway through university. His mother had died the previous year. He had already lost most of his family and didn't expect to live another decade. His father, Michael P. Kierkegaard, sent him on a holiday to Gilleleje, a fishing village about forty miles from Copenhagen. After a stern Christian upbringing, he was very vulnerable. Alone, taking hikes along the lovely countryside, he had what amounted to a religious experience. A heightened state of consciousness. A vision. He saw the idea that he was going to live and die for.

Back in my hometown I took long walks along the waterfront. I drove to Gros Cap and spent hours watching the Lake Superior waves break against the rocks. On weekends I stayed cooped up in my room reading and listening to Leonard Cohen albums. I drank up the black blood that kept me sane in a world that pursued its own interest. Sometimes I looked over the city and felt my sick soul. I thought of myself as a contradiction. One eye filled with women. One eye filled with night.

I worked in the same all-boys school I attended ten years back when I was a shy, acne-scarred kid. The tallest free-standing cross was still at the edge of the hill overlooking the city at the spot Père Marquette stood when he first beheld the rapids. Father Delaney, who used to be my Religion teacher, was the principal now. He hired me, an old boy, probably on the understanding that once a Catholic always a Catholic.

"We need guys like you, Markie-boy," he told me in his office. "To carry on the tradition. Teach me goodness, obedience, and knowledge, right?"

He hadn't changed a bit.

Neither had the school's smell. A combination of musty lockers and linoleum floors. Some of the same Basilians who had taught me were still there. The major difference were the new teachers, mostly former students like me, who were my age or older. Since the school was so small, with just over five hundred enrolled, the entire staff was in the same workroom with carrels against the wall.

I had a one bedroom apartment in a newer low-rise on the crest of the same hill overlooking the city and river. I lived frugally on my small salary. The bed and dresser were castoffs from my parents. The sofa I got second-hand. Only the TV and stereo were new – the first things I bought, along with the Chevalle, which was parked in the lot at the bottom of the hill.

Every week Lisa wrote from her own room at the university on the back of art postcards. She told me about her courses. She kept instructing me on art appreciation and visual perspective. This Rembrandt depicts the play of light and darkness. This Monet, which is too decorative for my tastes, can't be all bad. Why is our visual field so limited? She sent me parts of the Sunday *New York Times*, which wasn't available this far north. After only a few weeks I started to miss her. Her ripe body. Her little girl sighs when making love. Her full-bodied laugh. She was like an expanding lump in my chest, a weight that increased with each passing week.

I tried doing some work in the evenings, but I was too exhausted from teaching the boys the rudiments of English composition and the greatness of Shakespeare.

I sat on my balcony and looked over the city. Everything was visible. The steel plant. The International Bridge. What was left of the West End. The downtown core. My past life was a geography. Flashes of memory haunted me in my silence.

For some reason, snatches from the Baltimore Catechism would come to mind.

> Who made you?
> – God made me.
> Why did God make you?
> – To show forth His goodness and to be happy with Him forever in Heaven.

Once the cold autumn air came upon us there wasn't much to do. I coached football with another young teacher, Brian Dakota, who was from London. As the weeks passed, the cold winds got colder. The backlot of the school got chewed up. The rain gave way to wisps of snow. The multicoloured leaves had all disappeared. Lisa mentioned coming up for Thanksgiving, then changed her mind when an important project for school came up. We made plans for me to visit during Christmas break – and postponed her visit to April or May.

Every Sunday I ate at my parents' house under the bridge. Large meals that kept me going a day or two. Every Wednesday Brian and I went to Minelli's and had pasta dinners that got me through another few days. The rest of the week I subsisted on sandwiches and fruit.

Our football team made it to the city finals, where we lost on one play. I acted like a regular guy. I was a regular guy.

Brian and I decided to go out on a double date and get sloshed to drown our sorrows. I left it to Lori, Brian's girlfriend, to find me a date. She worked at City Hall. "Just make sure she has a sense of humour," I told her over the phone. "Looks too. Don't forget looks. And a brain. Don't forget that either. She has to be well-read. Might as well add money. Make sure she has an inheritance."

When I arrived at the Windsor, the three of them were waiting for me in the lounge. They sat on Victorian high-backed chairs and were sipping on white wine.

"Mark," Lori got up, "this is Janice Harcourt. She's a dietician with Public Health at City Hall."

I shook the hand of a pretty redhead with a toothy smile and freckled face. She looked like the girl next door, wholesome, athletic. Not bad looking at all, except she was a little too wide at the hips.

We made small talk. Then went to a movie next door at the Odeon. It was the same theatre I had tried to get into with a forged ID to watch Restricted movies. Everywhere I turned, it seemed, my past cinched me in like a straitjacket.

Every time I turned around I saw students, former friends I didn't want to meet, old buildings I didn't want to see.

Later we went to a new disco-bar down the street and settled in for a night of some good drinking. There was a dance floor and DJ and coloured lights. The music was Bee Gees and the bump.

Janice was quiet, even after a few drinks.

"What've you told her about me?" I asked Lori, when Janice had gone to the washroom.

"That you're egocentric. Think too highly of yourself. That you're vain. And not to take you seriously."

"Thanks a lot."

Lori was petite, with short ash-blond hair, blue eyes,

and a playful disposition. Brian was a broad-shouldered guy with sandy hair. He lifted weights, drove a half-ton, and made quality furniture on the side. His basement was filled with expensive carpentry tools he got from his father. He had a laconic sense of humour. My first year he had told one of my classes that I had served time in jail for aggravated assault. That had quieted the class for a long while.

"She also told Janice you're a fruit man," Brian snickered.

"I like fruit too," Janice told us later. "But I prefer them chopped up, and with a wide variety. With strawberries and kiwi and grapes especially. The kind that melts in your mouth."

"There you go, Trecroci," Lori piped in with a high squeal. "Someone really up your alley. Janice knows all about food and nutrition."

"Wait a minute," she said in earnest. "A dietician is different from a nutritionist."

"She's highly educated too," Brian said, smiling. "She's studied the philosophy of food management, the metaphysics of pizza-pasta consumption, and the evils of fast-food living."

"Cut it out, Brian," she looked sternly at him. "I don't joke about food. You are what you eat."

"Then Markie here's a fruit-head."

"There's a lot of sugar in fruit, you know," Janice leaned over to me. I smelled her perfume. It went right to my head.

We drank, danced a little, drank more, forgot about the coming winter, until we got completely silly.

At one point Lori took me away from the group and gave me a serious talking-to.

"I didn't tell Janice about Lisa," she said. "If anything comes of this, you're to tell her yourself. Is that understood? Janice is a nice girl. She deserves the best treatment."

I nodded, more than slightly inebriated.

Janice and I made plans to see each other again, while Brian and Lori were in deep conversation about something.

We went to movies. Sometimes dancing. One time to a play at the old Shingwaulk Hall put on by the university. Janice liked her fun, could talk, and had some conception of the wider world. She had travelled extensively with girlfriends. She was an avid reader and liked classical music, especially the singing of Pavarotti. She had despaired of ever finding anyone of refinement in the city, she told me. She had never had a serious relationship, she said. The clock was ticking.

"Not too much refinement, mind you," she added. "But someone whose idea of fun isn't getting sloshed on Friday night on beer after an Industrial hockey game."

"I know what you mean," I said, looking into her light blue eyes.

I liked her freckled soft skin and pouty lips.

In the four or so weeks of seeing her, though, I hadn't once made physical contact, except to dance with her.

"This city has the highest divorce rate in Canada, you know," she told me.

I was surprised to hear this. The way she explained it, the recent problems at the steel plant had caused a lot of people to be laid off. With nothing better to do, more and more people were hanging out at the local beer parlours, dancing some country, and screwing like rabbits.

"You can stick your country music," Janice added, as if it had left a bad taste in her mouth.

Towards the end of November the snow started to stay on the ground for longer periods of time. The northern winds howled outside my window. When I looked out over my balcony I saw the ice forming along the shores of the river, and my chest constricted. Winters had been fun as a kid. But they could be devastating if you didn't play hockey or ski. And if you were alone. S.K. called Copenhagen a cultural backwater, but at least he could take long walks, visit the theatre and the opera often. My city was worse than a cultural backwater. In the winter, without tennis, all I could do was stay in my room and watch TV.

One night, after another movie and drinks at the Windsor, Janice invited me up to her apartment. She had the upper floor of a wood-frame house at the edge of a park at the top of the hill. Not too far from my place.

She took my brown leather jacket and told me to sit down in the kitchen, where she served me tea and oranges.

During a lull, when we both couldn't find anything stupid to say, I gazed fixedly at her.

"What?" she said.

I shrugged in a theatrical fashion. There were no more lines. The script would take me where it wanted.

"What?" she said again.

I didn't make a move.

She took my hand and brought me to the living room, where it was dark. She had lighted a few candles and had a Pavarotti album going. Her perfume flooded my head. We sat on the floor on a duvet and immediately got into a clinch and kissed a bit. Her mouth tasted of oranges, with a lot of saliva. Full and soft. Nice.

"Why haven't you tried anything with me?" she asked, as I held her and she looked up at me with her large eyes.

Tell her about Lisa, S.K. whispered in my ear.

"I'm not looking for anything serious," I said.

"Who's looking for anything serious? In this city you're only looking for a little companionship. Someone who's simpatico. Someone who speaks the same language."

"Do we talk the same language, Janice?"

"Kiss me, you idiot."

We rolled on the duvet. She made a lot of noise. She was a deep moaner. There was a wild desperation in her responses.

After we discarded every piece of clothing, I had a good look at her. She was substantial, solid, wide at the hips, with smallish breasts, and a slim waist. She guided my hand to her lips, licked my fingers, and placed them between her legs.

"Touch me," she commanded, her voice husky, her manner careless of whatever persona she had fostered in the public eye.

She regained enough composure to ask if I had brought protection. I said no.

"Shit! I don't take the pill. You'll have to withdraw at the right time. Promise me you will."

"Sure," I said, hardly conscious, carried along by her take-charge attitude.

"Promise," she whined, her desire so intense she was scaring me. "Promise, promise, promise."

This begging, so unlike what I thought her to be, so naked and wanton, had changed her completely.

"I promise."

She got very excited. As I was inside her I could feel her melting, climbing the walls. I came over her stomach.

Afterwards she went immediately to the bathroom to wash up and came out in a bathrobe.

"Your turn," she said, as if we had been married for years. "You'll find the mouthwash in the cabinet."

I had never known such a hygienic girl. The mouthwash felt good in my raw mouth. I went back and joined her on the duvet. She put her head on my shoulder and trailed her finger over my abdomen.

"You've got a nice body," she said. "I really enjoyed that."

I looked at her reddish hair, the clean scalp under the roots. Her freckled skin. She was a human being, solid and substantial, very practical. Someone who knew how to take her pleasure with the least inconvenience. And she was very snugly. The wind was howling outside.

"You're being overly generous," I said.

"I get so carried away. I hope I didn't scare you."

"My knees are shaking."

"You're so facetious," she glanced up into my eyes. "I don't know if you're joking half the time."

"Listen, Janice," I began slowly. "There's something I have to tell you."

When I got to my car about an hour later, S.K.'s voice was loud and clear in my ears. You should have told her before making love, he chastised me. You're like the guy who samples everything women have to offer – with the proviso you're not buying. Your irony comes from superiority, not from humility. Your detachment is bogus. Your life will become an endless series of masks in an endless masquerade.

I've never been through the aesthetic stage, I told him. How can I know the world unless I know women? How can I know women unless I burrow in between their legs and make a nest for myself in their hearts?

Stupid fellow, he said. You're going the wrong way.

And don't forget. Your power is not that of a ruler or conqueror. It comes from your ability to hold yourself in check.

The northerly wind was blowing hard outside. The Chevalle sputtered a little, then came to life.

When I got back to the apartment the phone was ringing.

"I've been trying to call you all night," Lisa said, her tone curt and sharp. "Where have you been?"

"I was at Brian's house lifting weights. Watching some TV."

Lisa didn't like using the phone. She thought it cheated intimacy. It only made our separation harder to bear. She made the conversation short. She gave me details about my upcoming visit to the university. Then she paused.

"Is there anyone else in the room, Croach?"

"Of course not."

"You're breathing so heavily."

"I just came in from the cold. It's enough to take your breath away."

When I flew to Toronto for the Christmas break, Lisa was waiting for me at the airport. She cuddled up to me in the taxi to the university. I could smell paint on her. Her eyes were large with my presence.

"Missed me?" she said.

Living away from home had made her thinner. She seemed tentative, unsure of herself with me. I gave her a warm smile, my sins erased by her bounty.

The university was still relatively new in the north end of the city. But it had hired enough famous artists to have a solid graduate department in fine art. Somewhere in those bleak grey buildings, as well, were the offices of renowned poets.

She had a single room with bath in the graduate section of one of the new highrise residences. It was small and functional. We spent the day walking through the campus in our winter parkas. The functional concrete buildings had a raw look to them. Inside were the typical cafeterias, the student centres and library. A recent snowfall had left patches of snow in the hollow areas of the brown grass. The Fine Arts building where she had her classes was slanted and entirely walled with glass. She showed me the airy dance studios downstairs, the large open art studios upstairs, which were divided by partitions and lockers.

"The campus is hideous," she said, "except for this building. Thank God."

We ate in the cafeteria that was empty because of the

holidays, then went back to her room where she had stashed a few bottles of wine in her small fridge.

"Let's get drunk," she said, "to break the ice."

"Funny," I looked outside the window to the desolate wintry campus and farther to the open fields beyond the north boundary. "That's what they say up north too."

"Pardon me?"

"Sex and drinking are their only ways of staying warm from the cold."

She frowned. "I try to imagine how hideous it is for you up there. I tried to come up at Thanksgiving, honest. Listen," she brightened up, "I'm going to plan our trip to Paris, okay. For July. As soon as you finish your year. And I'll be up in May, as soon as I finish mine. You can hold on till then, can't you?"

"Of course. I have my books and my poetry to protect me. I am a rock. I am an island."

"You joke about everything," she said.

"It's the only way I can survive divided against myself."

"I don't know what you're talking about. Just don't fool yourself as well, Croach."

It only took us a few glasses of wine to get amorous. Lisa became excited. She had been waiting weeks for this moment, she said, honest to the core. She had resisted phoning so many times. Even the male models in art class had been getting her worked up, she confessed. She had refused numerous requests for dates. Even one of her teachers, some noted artist twice her age, had made a pass at her one evening after a party. They had been driving back to the campus in the back of a car. He was drunk, or pretending to be more drunk than he was. He had reached over and touched her breasts. But she had refused him without hurting his feelings. She was finished with that part of her life.

94

I listened with my mouth agape, and felt guilty.

When I got inside her I couldn't help comparing her with Janice. And then with Angela. They had gripped me down there in different ways, I thought – more inside myself than in her.

But, stupid me, I got lost inside myself at the crucial moment and withdrew from her.

I recognized my mistake too late.

Later, when we had cleaned up a bit and were lying side by side, Lisa gave me a quizzical look.

"You've never done that before."

"I forgot if you had resumed taking the pill," I said.

"I'm always on the pill, you know that. You can't go off and on, you know that."

"No, I don't know. It was just a spontaneous thing. Forget about it."

She remained quiet while I massaged the back of her neck.

"You felt so good," I said.

"Croach, have you been with another woman?"

"What? Are you kidding?"

"Just tell me if you have."

"You're kidding! You must be kidding."

She looked hard at me. I looked back.

She began to sob. She was sobbing and I was telling her to stop. But she wouldn't stop.

"We can't go on like this," she said, wiping her eyes. "It's too hard on me, Croach. You don't know. I feel too connected to you. I know I have to trust you up there. But it's been hard. You just have to get a job down here."

Her feelings overpowered me. I buried my face in her hair, sniffed her all over, brought my hand up and felt the contours of her skull.

"Haven't I tried?" I said.

"Then I'll have to drop out of school," she said. "Come to live with you up there."

"Don't be silly."

"I don't know," she shook her head. "Maybe we're headed in opposite directions. Don't you find it hard being away from me?"

"Yes, I do."

"You never mention it."

"What am I supposed to do? Mention it all the time?"

She gave me a tearful look. "I'm not as self-confident as you think I am, Croach."

"Neither am I."

"Are we talking about the same thing?"

"Look, what d'you want me to do?" I said, angry. "They're not hiring down here. And I hate doing substitute teaching. You're the one who went into the grad programme."

"It's not having children that's bothering you, isn't it? I can change my mind on that, you know."

"I'm not going to ask you to give up your work, Lisa."

"I can do both. I know I can."

We talked and talked, going around in circles, until I couldn't stay awake any longer.

The rest of the visit was marred by that first night. We went downtown to see a few movies, ate out at the Blue Cellar Room like old times, visited some galleries, made love as often as we could. "To squirrel up for the long winter," Lisa said. I saw how she turned men's heads. Her upright walk, her thin legs and great figure. Her attractive high forehead and piercing eyes.

Then for New Year's Eve we went to a party at Jon Halladay's place downtown.

The old regulars were there. Evelyn Chu and her girl-friend. Jon's girl, Bella Nardi. Some of the people from Lisa's class. And a few of Jon's actor friends. Jon had the upstairs floor of a two-storey brick house in a residential area north of the Danforth, in the Greek area. It was pop-ulated also by a smattering of actors and other artists, only a few subway stops from Yonge.

Some of us were in the living room, sitting on a mangy carpet or sprawled on the sofa, while the others were in the kitchen or the bedroom. Evelyn Chu was holding court in patched jeans and large pullover. The topic was the generation of the 1970s: success, selling out, and cyn-icism.

"I'm going to give the public what it wants, baby," Eve-lyn said, her voice high from too much vodka. "Look at Warhol. That's me. Warhol and Pop Art for the trashy masses who put the Beatles up there with Jesus H. Christ."

They asked me why I wrote. I had to think about it.

"For fame, fortune, and women," I said with a frozen smile.

"Bullshit," Evelyn swiped at the air. "Tell us the truth." She looked at Lisa. "Lisa, you tell us."

"He can speak for himself," Lisa said.

"But he never tells us anything. He's as close-mouthed as a muzzled dog. What're you afraid of, Mark Trecroci?"

"Ain't afraid of you . . . Chu."

"Oh, he's an evasive one, isn't he?"

At their exhibit in September she sold ten works, she said. It kept her in rent and food for six months. She had a plan to write a memoir of growing up in a Chinese home, being physically and mentally abused, turning to women for sexual solace, turning to drugs and prostitu-tion – all the absolute unvarnished truth.

"Just what the feminists want," she added, her lips curled down in defiance. "They'd lap it up like a sweet-oozing juice hole. I'd be a celebrity on the CBC. Then I could sell my artwork at a much larger price. Or make a movie on the ways of sexually satisfying a woman – ways men have no idea of. It would last as long as it took to have an orgasm."

This sparked a debate. Evelyn argued clitoral orgasms were the only orgasms. She challenged the women in the room to prove her wrong. Vaginal orgasms were a myth, she said.

"Aren't they both the same?" Bella Nardi spoke up. "Deep down, that is."

"Some women never even have orgasms," Evelyn said, disregarding her. "They don't know the power it gives them. Like creating a work of art. Building up to the moment of release. The moment when you become the work."

"Are you speaking as a woman . . . or as a man?" I asked her.

"I'm speaking as Evelyn Chu," she narrowed her eyes at me.

"But isn't Evelyn Chu part of something larger than herself? Something like a community? A gender? A family? Some larger whole she must answer to?"

"I answer to no one."

"But don't you make love to someone? Don't you want to connect?"

"Of course," she turned to her girlfriend, looking trapped.

"That's why I write," I told them. "To reconnect with a larger whole. To script the consciousness of people I've broken away from."

"That's baloney!" Lisa said. "You've made yourself into an observer, a recorder, Croach. You've detached yourself too much from what's natural. And you can't go back. You're unable to feel anything deeply any more. You've become an ironist."

I stared at her.

Evelyn's face brightened up. "Well, well," she said.

Afterwards I drank recklessly and avoided Lisa. If she was in the kitchen I'd be in the bedroom. If she was in the living room, I'd go into the kitchen. The hours slipped by. It was close to midnight. My head was swirling from having drunk Scotch and water. Couples started pairing off, as if to enter an ark.

I found myself, with five minutes to go, close to Bella in the kitchen. She had lost Jon.

"I don't know where he's gone off to," she said, not too sober herself. "The last time I saw him he said he had to run an errand. To get more dope or something. Where's Lisa?"

"She's talking to her friends in the living room."

"Whenever Jon and I fight we don't speak to each other for weeks. I don't know what's gonna happen with us, you know. Like, no offense, but you guys are too brainy for your own good. I don't know half of the things you're talking about. And when I think I do, you tell me you're only kidding. You wanna know what I think? I think there's only a limited amount of love in the world at any one time. And it's in short supply."

She focused in. Her words caught me by surprise. She had a little smile. Her large blue eyes bugged out at me. I stared at her lips, mesmerized by their liquid movements.

We heard the countdown from Times Square on TV in the other room. Then shouts that sounded like echoes of triumphant legions.

"Happy New Year!"

Bella naturally came into my arms for an innocent New Year's kiss. We hugged. I smelled her hair, the nape of her neck. I put my hands on her delicate bony back. Her shoulder blades felt like folded wings. She smelled of musky perfume.

I nibbled her ear. It was like soft fuzzy peach. She wiggled away and gave me her mouth. It was alive with hunger. At first it tasted foreign. A bit tarty like kiwi. But then it tasted like strawberry that had been mixed with wine. I was trying to suck her tongue out of her mouth.

Lisa walked in.

"Where's Jon?" Lisa said, her voice trembling. "He's certainly not with me! If he were with me maybe I'd play with his mouth too."

"I'm sorry," Bella said, breaking away from me.

"Don't play the little angel," Lisa barked at her. "I know for a fact that you're not."

I tried to slink away. There was a lot of racket close to the TV set in the other room. They probably thought we were celebrating the new year as well.

Bella rushed out of the room. Lisa's eyes burned into me.

"I don't see you for months!" she shouted. "I'm waiting in expectation for months!" She was shaking her head, working herself up into a frenzy. "What a fool I am. You've made me into a fool, Croach."

I had never seen her this angry. Her shouting silenced the other room. I slunk away.

By the time we were ready to go home it was too late to take the subway. Besides, we had drunk too much to be too steady on our feet. Evelyn Chu's girlfriend, who was sober, drove us back to the campus with Evelyn in the passenger seat. Lisa and I sat in the back quietly, chastened and spent. I could feel Evelyn gloating up front. I could feel her thoughts. Men, ugh! Forget about the vaginal orgasm.

At the residence Evelyn turned back to us as we were getting out.

"Want to come back to our place, Lisa?" she said, smiling wickedly.

"Maybe you can take him instead," Lisa said.

"No, he wouldn't do it for us."

"Very funny," I said.

As soon as we got into the room I said, "The last thing I want is to have a long talk."

She looked at me. "I can't believe what you've turned me into."

But the alcohol in our systems had its effect. Pretty soon we were cuddling and making up. Our love-making had a desperate edge to it, as if we had thrown away all pretence. Two opposites meeting and banging into each other.

Before I fell into a deep sleep, I faintly heard Lisa sobbing quietly and talking to herself.

12

I returned to the hard winter up north.

What makes us bad? I asked Kierkegaard. Inherent drives. Free will. And ego, he said. Mix them together and you've got one bad dude.

Each morning I'd wake up as if I had come back from the dead. I'd have my coffee and turn the radio on for the news as I prepared for school.

The Dallas Cowboys won Super Bowl XII. President Sadat of Egypt visited President Carter for peace talks. The Sandinistas of Nicaragua were preparing for civil war. Aldo Moro was kidnapped by the Red Brigades.

In the evenings I read and watched TV. I looked over the iced-in river. Saw the billows of coloured smoke over the steel plant. Was mesmerized by all the snow over the rooftops.

You're a walking contradiction, my godfather told me. You seek truth and you lie through your teeth. I'm an ironist, I answered. Don't fool yourself, he said.

After seven years of rejection letters and five other novels that hadn't panned out, my novel on Italian immigrants was accepted for publication. I was ecstatic for two days. I called Lisa. I made a dramatic announcement at school. I walked through the West End streets that were the setting for the novel.

Time had taken its toll. The West End had long ceased to be the thriving neighbourhood of ethnic stores and swarming kids on the sidewalks. I stared at the spot on the bridge where Perry had plunged to his death. I looked at the new building where the McFadden rink had once been. I viewed the ploughed-over land where the Stone Garden had centred the Eden of my youth.

The buildings and locations had ceased to exist, but the book would keep them alive. My sacrifices to the natural life had not entirely gone in vain.

My parents received the news with deadpan expressions that Sunday when I went over for dinner.

"But, Ma," I tried to joke with my mother in *dialetto* at the dinner table, "you're in the book. It'll make you famous."

"Don't get me mad," she swiped at the air before picking up a piece of bread. "*Sei pazzo!*"

She thought I was nuts. I had wasted my best years pursuing clouds. I could've become a lawyer or a doctor and started a family already. I was close to thirty, she repeatedly told me. And what had I done in life? Where was my house? Where was my family? Where were the things I could point to?

In her mid-fifties, she had aged into a stout woman with short red hair, a fair complexion, and an overly-critical disposition. No amount of fancy words was going to penetrate that peasant's sense of hard elemental facts. I wasn't even married. I was a disgrace.

My father was sitting at the head of the table in his thick plaid shirt and green work pants. His white hair was neatly brushed back. His lined attractive features were regarding me with suspicion.

"What did you say about us?" he said.

"It's only partly truth," I explained, avoiding his eyes.

"You mean you lied?"

"No, I didn't lie, but . . ."

"Well, you can say what you want, that's only the one thing."

"Look, I didn't lie, Dad. It's something called dramatic truth."

"Ah, you gave it a fancy name."

I tried to explain with my educated vocabulary that if I had stuck to the actual facts I would've written a historical document. The facts would've obscured the deeper meaning. Dramatic truth got to the heart of the matter quickly, the way actual truth never could. Besides, actual people had to be rendered larger than life, more intense and condensed in essence, to break the abstract medium of the printed page.

He stared at me. "*Vaffancul'*," he said. "You lied."

We ate the rest of the meal in silence. I glanced at my father every so often when he wasn't looking.

I had fought him all my life. Along with his Italian background. His lack of education. His uncouth ways. And his ridiculous ideas. Ever since the Italian trip, however, I had come to admire him. His immigration. His work ethic. I had made myself his English voice, his myth-maker. A myth had to take liberties with the facts to get at the meaning behind the facts, I reasoned with myself. The old myths had been shattered, but not their messages. It was time for a new garb for those old messages. A myth-maker had to sacrifice his natural life for the truth. Fill himself with black blood and pour it out on the page.

My father had mellowed with age. He had come to accept his lot in life. He saw the value of his job since the accident to his back. He saw himself more as a success at the head of his family. The only remaining worry was to get Lianna and me married so that he could become a grandfather.

To him, my job at the school was a step forward. My mythmaking was a step backward.

"When am I going to see this girlfriend from Toronto?" he asked me. "She's been up here, and we've never seen her."

"You always told me, Dad. Never bring a girl here unless I'm going to marry her."

"Yeah, that's right."

"Okay, later in the summer, okay?"

"I hope you're serious this time, that's only the one thing."

"He'll never get married," my mother scoffed. "He has his head in the clouds."

At least Janice was excited for me. We went out on a double date with Brian and Lori to celebrate. To a disco-bar on the city's main drag.

"How was your trip?" Janice asked me, while Brian was dancing with Lori. She had been glum the whole evening. I hadn't called her upon returning, letting the weeks go by to make some sort of separation from Lisa.

"Fine," I said.

"Did you sleep with her?"

"Come on, Janice," I snapped my face away. "If you want to talk about that, the evening's not going to last very long."

"I'm happy over your book," she said, and remained in a tense silence the rest of the night.

When I drove her home later, she didn't invite me up and I didn't insist.

"You gotta choose," she said. "Call me when you're ready," she slammed the door in my face.

The publication of the book helped me to get through the winter. I looked over the city a new person. The snow and the familiar landmarks weren't as confining. They had been transformed into a mythical kingdom.

About three weeks later, the door bell rang late one Friday and there was Janice, dressed in a cashmere turtleneck and denims, tears streaming down her face, her red hair aflame.

"You shit!" she cried out.

I stood back, impassive, unable to move a muscle.

"Who do you think you are?" she said. "Look at what you've done to me? Are you happy, huh?"

But as soon as she stepped in, her anger wilted. She leaned her head on my shoulder. I couldn't resist putting my arms around her. Her body, that of a woman in distress, was an offering that I couldn't refuse.

I made love coldly, however. As a sort of punishment. She was my hometown that I hated and loved, the place where I had been formed, the place of my actual truth.

Afterwards, she was quiet and docile. She cuddled up, stayed close and snug, made sighs short and infrequent, and drifted off to sleep.

I couldn't sleep at all. My feverish mind was like a monkey jumping back and forth on the same branches.

The next morning she got up early. I managed to get an hour of sleep while she was out. When I woke up it was a sunny Saturday, the dazzling light off the snow flooding the apartment. Janice had gone out to get some food. The table was set with a gigantic breakfast. Grapefruit. Oatmeal. Eggs. Toast.

She was beaming as I approached the table in a groggy state of mind.

"This is what you need to start the day," she said, beaming from ear to ear. "A substantial breakfast. All the nutrients to keep you going the whole day. *Buon appetito*."

We resumed our dating. Movies. Cross-country skiing. Amateur theatre. Jaunts across the river to the Michigan side. Except now, she was making me elaborate meals, using her expertise as a dietician. They were tasty and nutritious, I had to admit. She watched me eating with genuine pleasure.

One time she took me to dinner to meet her parents. They were kindly British types. They looked me over like an upstart while they served tea. Janice never again broached the subject of Lisa. It wasn't long before the snow started melting.

Every day, it seemed, my daemon spoke to me. I walked the Copenhagen streets with him. Listened to his ideas. Gave him a few of mine. He wore a large-brimmed hat. Had a frock coat and spectacles. A stick figure with his umbrella. His large protuberant mouth smiled or scowled at me. He had such bad teeth. He smelled of stale yogurt and tobacco.

I considered taking some evening courses at the local university, a small school that was affiliated with Laurentian in Sudbury. Its Philosophy Department consisted of one teacher, a Karl Scheler, a second-generation German from Alberta. I spoke to Scheler on a few occasions in his office in the former Shingwauk Hall. A meticulous man with wavy hair and a kindly disposition, he was more than willing to talk philosophy. He knew S.K. well enough but was better versed on Kant and Hegel and Heidegger.

"Read Heidegger," he told me. "He's Kierkegaard's true successor."

"Wasn't he an academic like Hegel?"

"Yes," he lowered his eyes, "but who of us can really live our philosophy?"

I took on my daemon's voice. I've produced an illusory theatre of pseudonymous authors, I told Scheler. Each author contributes an argument and then leaves the stage. Like a Socratic Theatre Company, I added. The awakened man is he who senses the weightiest aspect of life – the openness to infinite possibilities. Consciousness swings precariously between its finite givenness and its infinite possibilities, as if on a trapeze without a net. The reflective man keeps swinging. No wonder vertigo results, I said. Not to mention dread. Fear and trembling. And despair.

Scheler listened to me with a tight smile.

The seeker wants an intensification of life, a concentration of consciousness that makes life larger, richer, denser, than our ordinary natural lives.

The mythmaker moves back and forth from the outside of the old collective myths to the inside of his own private visions. He must live in both worlds. Invisible in one and strong in the other.

The days of Ernest Hemingway were over, I told Scheler. Hemingway had participated in the collective myths. In the wars. The bullfights. The fishing and hunting expeditions. In the codes of the heroic warrior. And then he had recounted them in a biblical style, reinforcing their deep sources in the collective unconscious. Now we had to look at the mundane, the quotidian, I told Scheler. We had to fashion a new mythology that satisfied the head and the heart. That healed the old wounds.

Karl Scheler nodded like a mute psychiatrist letting me reveal all my black blood.

As I walked past the portables outside the main building, I wondered if I had revealed too much. Had Scheler understood me? Did he think I was mad? Who did I think I was, proclaiming on Ernest Hemingway? Yes, he had been a godfather of mine, but I was as far from Hemingway as a guy could get. Daily I died the death of a coward. In my anxieties. In my inner life. Daily I did nothing but mope and read and watch TV. I didn't drink excessively. I didn't go out deep-sea fishing or big-game hunting. I didn't get my legs hit by shrapnel. Didn't live in Paris with the great artists of the 1920s. Didn't do anything of great merit and stature. And then go over the catwalk in back of the colonial house in Key West to the loft over the pool house and write out the great sentences that would get me millions of dollars.

Nobody would know about me. Nobody would care. Did I have the spirit to forge on regardless?

And could I do it with Lisa? Or did I have to be invisible to my own wife as well?

Lisa's letters arrived at my place with a regularity that surprised me. They were full of art instruction, anecdotes about her student life, her anticipation over her visit and our trip to Paris in the summer.

On the back of a Willem de Kooning from the Tate Gallery:

I wonder what this separation will mean for us in the long run? I know that it's very difficult for you up there, what with the cold and the isolation. I'll try to put some warmth in these letters, but it isn't easy for me. Sometimes I forget for long stretches of time that you even exist, and these letters are a means of bringing you back to life. The phone just doesn't work as well because we're too awkward and it's painful to hear your voice and only get so little of you. I've never liked the phone for that sort of thing, as you well know. With a letter I can relax and put my entire thought on you and formulate my response. Letters are much more intimate, Croach, believe me. I feel I'm giving myself to you much moreso than if we were talking on the phone. And our words won't be lost, will they? I can read over your letters whenever I want. I feel I have you with me whenever I need you.

I had to get used to you not being here, you know, and I had to stop thinking about sex because that would only upset me. When I become a non-sexual being I put my whole energy into my work and it's amazing how the canvases take on a new tension, as if I can literally transpose my hunger onto a flat surface. I do miss you a lot, though, and would rather have you beside me in bed.

Keep well, Croach. I hope you can find some warmth in your life up there.

This letter upset me so much I refused to see Janice. Lisa took on new stature in my eyes. I felt totally unworthy of her. She was so much grander than me. More loyal. With more dedication to her work. It was odd. The longer I was with her, the smaller she became in my eyes. And the longer I was away from her, the larger she became in my eyes.

I didn't answer the phone. I lived at the school, gave my whole energy to the students, came home like a zombie, and fell exhausted onto bed. I tried to snatch some time in the evenings to do some writing, but I was usually too exhausted to accomplish much.

Then in early April I picked up the phone one evening and it was Bella Nardi. She was in town visiting her aunt and uncle and wanted to meet for drinks.

At the Windsor she looked very different than she did in Toronto. She was in a low-cut red cardigan and tight black pants that revealed her slim sexy figure. Her dark hair was swept back and her eyes were large on her sharp features.

We hugged warmly. She smelled of musk and lavender soap. It went right to my head.

It seemed strange to me that Jon wasn't interested in marrying her – a topic that I broached delicately after we got through the initial chatter.

"I don't know," she said, sipping on a glass of wine. "Marriage would tie him down too much. An artist doesn't get married. He lives with different women for the rest of his life. What about you and Lisa?"

"Good question," I said.

We lapsed into silence.

"I have to tell you something and I don't like doing it," she said later.

I waited.

She played with her glass. "It's not fair that I'm the only one who knows."

"Either you tell me or you don't."

She furrowed her brows and pursed her lips. I had already stepped back, watching it unfold before me.

She told me that Lisa and Jon had a thing going last year. I acted shocked. Yet, after some time, it became apparent I was deeply hurt.

"When last year?" I asked her.

"Oh, I don't know exactly," Bella said. "Last winter, I guess, when they were working towards that group exhibit."

I quickly calculated it was before the New York trip.

"How did you find out?" I said.

"Jon told me. He wanted to prove how tough he was. You figure this out. He wanted to prove he wasn't worthy of me, he said."

It made perfect sense to me.

"I can't figure these artists out at times," she said, shaking her head.

Two nights later I took Bella to a country and western tavern farther up Queen, where the chances of seeing Janice or her friends were slim. We sat in the dim recesses of a corner, while a local band with a lead singer who must've been fifty years old went through the old favourites. A few couples in denims and flowered shirts were up on the dance floor, doing their best to follow the steel guitars and yodels. A couple of natives from the Garden River Reserve sat at the bar guzzling beer.

The place was so dingy and drab you had to have hidden sources of self-confidence not to feel depressed.

I told Bella I used to go to places like this when I was in my early twenties. To search out loose women. I had been so desperate I would've screwed the ugliest one who offered herself.

"You're kidding," Bella looked at me.

"No guff," I said.

Stupid me, though. All I did, I went on, was sit at a table all night sipping on beer while these middle-aged couples danced and conversed drunkenly, the cigarette smoke and beer fumes finally defusing my lust.

Bella drank a rum and coke while I gulped down gin and tonic.

"What a pathetic place," she said.

I tried to make silly conversation. I talked about the latest TV shows, music albums, movies, all the things every other couple would speak about. Bella answered in monosyllables, her mood deteriorating by the minute.

"Why did you bring me here?" she asked me.

"This was my life. Tell me about your life."

She didn't feel up to it, I could see. Her lips cut into each other to show her displeasure with me. She had been born and raised in the Italian section of Toronto, she said.

112

Her father was a construction worker, her mother a housewife. She had played volleyball and run track in high school. There had been a few boyfriends of the Gino variety, who had tried to get her barefoot and pregnant. She studied History and Geography at university. Had a short affair with a married professor. Studied to become a teacher. Was still looking for a full-time job. Met Jon Halladay at a party given by his brother, an Art teacher at one of her former schools.

"I'm just looking for a little beauty," she shrugged. "What can I say? It's nothing to write home about, I know. I just want the normal things any girl would want. A good man to love and children to make that love holy."

I looked at her.

At that moment we were distracted by a commotion close to the bar. Some dark-skinned guy in a coloured shirt who was drunk was shouting at the two natives at the bar who were trying to ignore him. I looked closer at the guy and recognized him.

It was the Blackman, Pasquale Salerno, who used to pick fights with the popular guys at the McFadden rink during our high School years. Though he had put on weight and lost some hair, he was doing the same thing as fifteen years ago. How could I ever mythologize him?

"Let's get outta here," I said to Bella.

As we slipped out, the Blackman got up abruptly, dislodging his chair, and stalked up to the bar. One of the natives pulled out a knife.

I caught the action in the corner of my eye. The native made three quick swipes in the air. It happened so quickly the Blackman stood there in shock, bleeding in delayed time. The natives left before he could react. We beat them to the door.

As we were driving out of the parking lot we spotted Pasquale on the sidesteps of the tavern, cursing his head off. A woman was beside him trying to stop the bleeding. The natives had slipped off into the night and the Black-man was cursing into the dark sky.

"I can't believe it," Bella said in the car.

I felt despondent. The mythical kingdom had regained its squalid roots.

"What the fuck are you trying to tell me?" she said.

I brought her to the trendy disco-bar on Queen which I frequented with Brian and Janice. We had a few drinks and danced a few numbers. But the evening was beyond repair.

"Take me home," Bella said, not long afterwards.

In the car back to her uncle's place in the West End I was silent.

"Are you mad at me for telling you about Lisa?" she said.

"No, I'm just sick at heart."

"I don't understand."

"There's nothing to understand. Except we can never escape our pasts. And the invisible world is the only true world."

"You're a real downer, aren't you?"

"Correct me if I'm wrong," I said. "But if a woman is angry at a guy, she physically can't screw him, right?"

"Pardon me?" she raised her voice.

"A woman can't make love with a guy she's angry with. It's a physical impossibility. She can let the guy have his way and everything, but she can't give herself to him."

"I don't know what you're talking about. Just drive me home, okay. I've had enough of artist types for a while, I'll tell you."

I was quiet the rest of the way. The West End was darker than ever, with fewer street lights. Dark patches of snow like miniature dirty sand dunes hugged the sidewalks.

Bella got out of the car and slammed the door.

Who knew? Maybe I let the best of them all get away. Maybe I had sensed the sadness in the pit of her own soul. Maybe I had changed the lines in the soap opera intrigue. Maybe I just had to show some restraint, as S.K. continually advised me.

And then maybe I didn't know what the hell I was doing.

13

Lisa finally came up for a visit on a Friday in the middle of May.

The sky was deep blue, with intermittent puffy clouds. As soon as her dark form exited the plane she seemed to draw the light to her, intensify it, and shine it back. We hugged and kissed awkwardly in the arrival area. I drove her from the airport, past the great hulk of mills of the steel plant, right to my apartment, where we were on the bed as soon as we could slip out of our clothes.

"I have to get used to you again," she said. "You're like a stranger."

Indeed, her body felt and tasted very different than I remembered in New York and Toronto. Had she changed, or was it me? The lingering odour of paint thinners on her skin lessened my ardour.

"Lisa," I said later, as she was unpacking, "could you do me a favour? Could you please start using some skin cream or scent, or something like that?"

She looked at me, not quite sure what I was saying, until it dawned on her. She made a few swipes at the air as if fanning away smoke.

"Sure, if you want," she said, with hurt in her voice.

Before, when she had come up, it had been during the holidays, I told her. Either Christmas or the March break. Now she'd be virtually chained to the apartment the whole two weeks of her visit. She had no car at her disposal. I'd be away at school. She'd be quite isolated.

"Let's not talk foolishness," she said, regaining her spirits. She went to the kitchenette. "I brought a few books. I'm back to reading Emily Carr. Plus, I can walk, can't I? Where's the frying pan? I'll make you an omelet to kill all omelets. Break a few eggs, make love again, and it'll be as if we've never been apart the past few months. I've been so looking forward to coming up here, Croach."

She was nervous and excited, filled with a charged energy that was infectious.

I drove to the closest mall to get a few things, including wine. We had a late dinner with candle light close to the sliding doors at the balcony. Off in the west, over the plant, the large setting sun painted the sky. In mid-May the city became alive with greenery and lilac. Buds sprouted, peeking through the hard northern soil, bracing themselves for the cool evening breeze.

"I've always liked this view," she said, looking over the city and the river.

I told her how the acceptance of the Italian book had refashioned the city in my eyes. I was above it, both literally and figuratively, I told her. The hockey arena wasn't just the hockey arena. The International Bridge wasn't just the International Bridge.

"Perspective, you mean?" she said. "Emily Carr got to the point where she was painting the spirit of a cabin rather than capturing it log by log."

"Yeah, perspective. But don't you ever feel at times there's a destiny at work in your life? And that you only catch a glimpse of it in recollection?"

"We make our own destiny, Croach," she laughed.

"As if we're part of something way bigger than ourselves. As if we're just these little waves, bobbing up and down."

"Jeez, the book's swelled your head even more."

"I'm talking about self-abnegation."

"And I'm talking self-importance. Don't get religious on me, Croach," she flipped her hair back and sipped more wine. "The problem with you is that you think too much. Like me at times. Abstractions only make us turn away from the things themselves. We lose the freshness of vision."

"I don't think that reality is in the things themselves. They're transitory. Mutable. They're only shadows of the real."

"That sounds like Plato. So where's the real?"

"In our heads," I smiled.

"I'd rather live at my nerve ends. In the here and now."

"But how're you going to recapture the freshness of these fleeting moments?"

"You're so worried about losing the moments," she laughed, "that you're losing the moments."

"Understand life backwards, but live it forwards, right?"

"Do me a favour, Croach," she shook her head. "I don't want you to remember me. All the time you were away from me I was trying to remember you. Now that I have you in front of me I don't want to remember you. I can't bear to be away from you, don't you understand that?"

She walked around to my side of the table. She took my head and hugged me to her waist. "I missed you so much," she said.

The strength of her feelings embarrassed me.

"Croach, listen to me," she said. "We can't be separated again for that length of time, okay? Promise me."

My ear was to her stomach. I could hear gurglings,

fleeting echoes of digesting food, in the deep recesses of her body.

"I'm dying up here," I whispered. "I can't talk to anyone."

"I thought you liked silence."

"But not too much."

"I heard from Jon that Bella Nardi was up here," she said. The hint in her voice was unmistakable.

"She told me you and Jon had a thing going last year. Before the New York trip."

She stiffened, digested the words, and stepped away from me.

"That's not true," she said.

"Was she lying to me?"

"I'm not saying that."

"It's either-or, Lisa."

"Not necessarily," she said, facing the city behind the sliding doors. "But you have to decide that."

I remained silent. She paused and took in a few long breaths, as if sucking up the oxygen for a long ordeal.

"Last year, in February, Jon and I were in the studio just chatting after a long day of work. I was on the sofa with a blanket over me because it was so cold. We had a little wine, I admit, to keep warm. At one point Jon was handing me another glass and he kissed me. I guess he caught me at a very vulnerable moment. I hadn't seen you in months. And I must've been weak. We ended up making love, yes, but it only happened that once. I told him, immediately afterwards, that it wasn't going to go any further than that. I told him you wouldn't approve."

I looked at her.

"I don't know what he told that bitch, but that's the way it happened, believe me."

I stared at the table, the empty wine bottles, the dirty dishes, the remnants of our meal.

"Say something," she said.

"What d'you mean, I wouldn't approve?"

"It's just an expression."

"That I wouldn't like it? That I'd approve under different circumstances? That I was your keeper?"

"Okay, okay," she was sniffling. "Okay, you made your point." She was crying. "I'm sorry, okay. I'm only human."

The moment came right there to confess about Janice. I could feel it come up like a big fat balloon. But if I changed the topic, it would take away from her moment. It was her time – except she hadn't confessed. She had been found out.

I told her about Bella's visit instead. The tavern fight. The disco-bar. The ride back to her aunt's place. I laid it on thick.

"She was after you, wasn't she?" Lisa said. "The bitch. But you know what, Croach? I wouldn't blame you if you had slept with her. Believe me."

"You wouldn't've minded?" I said.

She took out a cigarette from her knapsack, lit it, and fanned away the smoke. The action seemed so mannered, so studied, that it knocked me off kilter.

"No," she said. "Not if I knew you really cared for me. Not if I knew we were going to spend the rest of our lives together."

Christ, I felt I was in a play, stepping into my part every so often, then stepping out and observing.

"Okay, okay, listen," I suddenly got up and paced the floor. "Let me bring you into the reality of my life here. I get up each morning and go to work. I teach teens the rudiments of literature. This is a symbol. This is a metaphor. The primary task is to keep them from nodding off in boredom. Or keep their discipline in check. I come home exhausted. I live most intensely on the inside, in the invisibility of my head. I converse with my ghosts, past and present. I do a little reading, watch TV, and go to bed. This is my life up here. On the outside I feel I'm in this vast drama, sleepwalking through everything."

"It must be hideous, Croach," she shook her head. "But how can I help you?"

"I don't think anyone can, that's just the thing. I'll always be alone in the things that matter the most to me."

"Don't say that. You know you can share them with me."

I shook my head. "I don't know."

"You can talk about anything with me, you know that."

She was right. I'd be able to talk with her for hours on end. About my godfathers. About my work. About her work. About anything.

Later we moved to the sofa. We talked about other matters. For hours.

It was two in the morning.

"Lisa, let's go to bed," I said.

She smiled and kissed me. "You want me to wear perfume?"

"It's up to you," I said. "We're going to my parents for Sunday dinner. They want to meet you."

With that she gave me a big hug.

By the time I was in bed beside her I was exhausted. All that talking had emptied me so much that the voices of all my inner ghosts had been put to rest. It took me about ten seconds to gain oblivion.

14

In the first book he ever published, my godfather maintained that the ironist achieves a detachment, or what he called an estrangement, from everything around him. A gap wedges itself between his inner life and his outer life. Immediacy is lost. People around him begin to look like puppets on a string. He himself feels like a puppet.

To get to the house under the bridge we drove down the hill to Queen and headed for the West End.

"Let's go over it again," Lisa said.

She was in a black outfit with dress slacks, her hair brushed back, her fine features outlined with a bit of makeup. I could smell the scent of lilacs on her.

"My father's a millwright at the steel plant," I said. "He likes hunting and fishing, playing bocci, and playing cards. My mother's an ordinary housewife who doesn't speak English. She's never learned to drive. You have to be careful with her. She's a born critic. My father's okay, but don't get into a political discussion with him. Don't tell him your parents were Communists, for one."

"If you say so," she made a face. "I'm very nervous, Croach."

"They're more nervous than you. You're the first girl I've ever brought home to see them."

"Thanks. That makes me even more nervous. I've never even met your sister."

"That's just circumstances."

Lianna had been working in Toronto for over a year at

an insurance company. She roomed with another Soo girl. It would've been good to have her as a buffer between my parents and Lisa.

To my parents Lisa was the "painter in Toronto." The girl still in school. The girl I had met in Italy. The girl who had replaced the "other girl." She was as unreal as a character in one of my books.

"A painter?" my father asked me once. "What does she paint?"

"Modern art."

"Modern art? Like that picture in the TV room there?"

Their idea of art was kitsch landscapes and furry little animals bought at department stores. My mother had two expensively framed pictures of cats – one in her bedroom, one in the kitchen. My father had a treacly landscape of purple mountains and a small brook in a never-land forest in the "TV room."

"Whatsa matter?" my mother asked me once in *dialetto*. "Why don't you get a girlfriend in this city? Are you ashamed of us?"

"How would you speak to her, Ma?" I said.

"We would speak, don't you worry, *figlio mio*."

We approached the International Bridge that sloped down over the street. Above it, over the rise of the tracks that also traversed the street, we could see the highest point of the steel plant. It was the top of the new giant blast furnace with its flame at the crown.

"Look at that!" Lisa said. "That's amazing. I'll bring my camera next time. It's like a Statue of Liberty."

"It's more a statue of toil and woe," I said.

"This is where you grew up?" she said.

We passed the entrance to the locks, the bridge plaza, the abandoned chrome plant, and came closer to the hulking silhouette of the steel plant that rose above the neighbourhood roofs like a black castle.

"Yes," I said. "It's the last place you'd expect a literary giant to have his roots."

"It's fascinating," she said. "Look at that old paper mill. And the skyline of the mills. And the train tracks underneath the green girders of the bridge."

For a moment I tried to see it all in her fresh eyes.

"Right," I said. "You didn't have to grow up here. You didn't have to take the constant traffic from the bridge right over your window, the thick smoke from the pulp mill, the rattle of the boxcars."

"I'm entitled to my perspective."

"Sure you are."

"Don't be upset, Croach."

We came to rest in the paved driveway of the two-storey wood-frame house with the turquoise imitation brick siding. My parents greeted us awkwardly at the back, where they were sitting waiting for us on lawn chairs on the cement patio. Over the garage to the south loomed the hulk of the paper mill and the piles of logs, all of which blocked the sight of the locks. The back garden stretched now all the way to the parking lot of the Verdi Hall. Sprouts peeped out of the well cared-for soil. There were a number of other back gardens, all neatly tended, of the other Italian families on the short street.

We were all very awkward. My mother shyly looked Lisa over, definitely impressed. I looked at her with my mother's eyes. Her black statuesque form. Her dark hair gleaming. Her totally alert eyes. There was an utter aliveness about her that couldn't help drawing attention to itself.

I was tongue-tied. It was as if my future world had met my past world.

Finally Lisa looked over the garden. "What've you planted, Mr. Trecroci?"

"Call me Nico, please. Come with me. I will show you, Lisa."

He was clearly impressed with her as well.

While they walked over the wooden slats down the centre of the garden my mother gave me a look of incredulity.

"Where did you get *her*?" she said in *dialetto*.

"I found her in a church, Ma," I said, smiling, trying to make a joke in my imperfect Italian.

"She looks a little . . . too much for you, *figlio mio*."

I laughed. "You're joking, Ma, of course."

"Can she cook?"

"Yes. Very well too."

"Better than me?"

"No, no, of course not."

"And she's an artist?"

"She's back in school now, but she hopes to paint, yes."

"Is she Catholic?"

"No, Ma, she's not."

"What is she?"

"Ma, I'm not even Catholic anymore."

"You work at a Catholic school, don't you? Is she baptized?"

"I don't think so, no."

A frown crept over her features. It developed into a deep scowl.

"She'd have to get baptized," my mother said under her breath.

"Ma, we're just visiting for Sunday dinner, for Chrissakes."

"And the kids, they'd have to be baptized."

"Ma – !"

When my father and Lisa came back, they were in deep conversation about growing tomatoes, how tricky it was and how they needed tender loving care.

"My parents had a back garden when I was a kid," Lisa explained.

Then down in the basement, as we ate the homemade pasta with roasted chicken and baked potatoes, Lisa started talking about our visit to Italy. How much she enjoyed the Italian cuisine, the Italian architecture and art, and the great people who were so friendly.

"It's so fantastic there," she said. "The light is dazzling. I learned so much about art and seeing things in a new perspective. And, of course, I met Marco there too."

My father was beaming from ear to ear.

"What does your father do?" he asked her.

"He's retired now. But he used to work the printing press at a newspaper."

"He's a working man, then?"

"Oh, yeah, he believes in the working man. The working man's the heart and blood of any country, he used to tell me."

"Here, have more wine," he poured for her.

"It tastes great. Very full bodied."

My father's smile got larger. I was eating and observing, watching her work her charm on him. My mother ate quietly, throwing me a scowl every so often. I was afraid, if I wasn't vigilant enough, that she'd throw a glass of water over Lisa's head and baptize her then and there.

During the dessert and coffee Lisa brought up her interest in trekking the Bruce Trail and the bush. My father invited her out on a fishing trip the next weekend.

"Nico!" my mother interjected. "She doesn't wanna go fishing!"

"*Sì, sì*," Lisa smiled at my mother. "*Voglio andare pescare. Voglio vedere il bosco di* Lake Superior. I want to see the bush where the Canadian painters went."

My father's face was in seventh heaven. She was too good to be true.

He took her into the cantina afterwards to show her his wine-making equipment. Lisa marvelled at his workbench. He made it himself, he said, right after finishing the basement out of two-by-eights and four-by-fours reinforced with large bolts. Over it in the corner were all the carpentry tools and jars of nails and screws and whatnots he had accumulated over the years.

"I wish I had something like this at my studio. This is simply marvellous, Nico. Everything at your fingertips. And all neatly arranged."

"I like to make and repair things," he said. "See this house. I rebuilt it myself over the years. Bit by bit. It took a long time. You should've seen it when we first moved in. Marco didn't want to live here. But we worked at it. He helped me too."

"That's why you couldn't move out, wasn't it?" she said.

"It's our home."

"You look at it a different way when you make it yourself."

He looked at her and smiled.

It embarrassed me. I looked up at his fishing rods hooked onto the ceiling in between the exposed beams. At my old racquets and baseball bats and other sports equipment they'd never throw out. His work clothes hung to the right of the doorway. On the other side was the cupboard he had made for his hunting rifles. Then the shelves of preserves, cupboards for large quantities of flour and pasta. The freezer. And of course the wine bottles in slots in the far corner, with the huge demi-johns, and the slatted wine press.

"Just like the one at your sister's farm in Italy," Lisa remarked, her eyes not missing a thing.

Later he took her to his other work bench in the garage, a larger replica, with the same arrangement of tools and a clock-radio. There was an electric saw, a small electric heater for the winter months, and an aluminum boat and motor.

"I like to get out of the house sometimes," he said, giving her his bashful grin.

I followed behind their tête-à-tête, an unneeded translator in this meeting of the two heads of state of my two worlds.

He showed her the mounted duck wings he'd amassed over the years, the citations from various states for returning ankle bands, the photographs of fishing expeditions, some going back to my high School years.

"Dad, she's seen enough," I said.

"Don't be ridiculous, Croach," she gave me a tight smile.

"I just go for the duck and game birds," he said. "Not for deer or anything like that. It just passes the time. And fishing . . . you know, my friends in Pesaro, they were the big fishermen in their boats in the Adriatic, while I worked on the farm, you see. That's only the one thing."

"Your sister's farm was fantastic," Lisa said.

She went into the particulars of the visit to zia Gina's farm in Pesaro. How we had harvested the grapes and apples. The visit to the market. The slaughter of the pig.

The names of everyone. Milena. Gasparo and Tomasso.
Zio Giovanni with his cap.

My father's eyes were watering.

"I had to leave all that," he said, his voice choking. "We
couldn't make enough from our farm. I had to travel to
Germany to work. I had to play the accordion at dances. I
had to become a factory worker. It made a lot of problems
when I first came to Canada."

We strolled out of the back of the garage into the garden. The sun was low over the plant skyline. The red sandstone of the paper mill gathered the dark. We could hear
the faint rumblings of trains and the pit-pat of falling logs.
A pleasant breeze ruffled our clothes. We could see part of
the new waterfront downtown and the large cross overlooking the city on the hill.

"It's supposed to be the tallest free-standing cross in
North America," I said.

"It's too bad you don't see the garden in July and
August," my father told her. "When everything's ripe. The
tomatoes and green beans. The zucchini and cucumbers.
The raspberries at the back there. The squash and sun-
flower plants. And all types of lettuce too."

"Maybe after our trip to Paris, uh Croach? We can
spend some time here."

"You're going to Paris?" my father said in surprise.

"Yeah, hasn't Mark told you?"

My father gave me a pained expression. "That's good.
That's good. I got around a lot before and after the war,
you see. Germany, mostly. Yugoslavia during the war. But
I always wanted to travel more. To see Paris and London.
Maybe even Egypt and Greece."

"Why didn't you?" Lisa said.

"My wife, she's not much for the travelling."

"You have to go back to Italy, Dad. They were asking about you all the time. You can afford it. Why don't you go? Alone, if you have to."

"Yeah, maybe I'll go. It's been a long time since we left. It's changed so much. Sometimes I'm afraid to go back, I have to tell you. You've left that part of your life behind you, see, and you've changed so much. That's only the one thing." He gave me a wry grin. "Why, I bet even the language has changed, hey, Marco." He picked up a handful of black rich soil. "Do they still call this *la merda di Dio?*"

"No, no one calls it the shit of God anymore," I translated for Lisa's benefit.

"It's funny, isn't it?"

"Yeah," I said. "In New York we saw this exhibit, in a gallery, Dad. Of black soil inside a room. It covered the floor."

"I don't understand," he frowned. "Why would they do that?"

"Look at your house, Nico," Lisa stared at him. "Why does it mean so much to you? Because you lived here so long and worked on it so much, right?"

"Yeah, I guess so," he arched his eyebrows.

"The same with the soil. Somebody worked on it. Put it in a new place so others could look at it in a new way. That way it might regain its value."

"But the soil is for growing things," he said.

"That's right," she smiled. "That's why you value it so much."

"I don't know," he shook his head, "it sounds stupid to me, that's only the one thing."

On the drive back to the apartment, Lisa sat close to me and cuddled up.

"Your parents aren't so different from mine, you know.

They're very down-to-earth. And you're so much like your father, Croach, I can't believe you've become so different."

"You're kidding."

"Your mannerisms are very much the same."

"No way."

She settled back against the seat and took in a big breath. "Sometimes I think we're only trying to be better versions of our parents, no matter what we think."

I thought about that.

"I can't believe you wanna go fishing," I said later.

"Hey, why do you think I'm up here? I wanna see some of the Algoma country too, you know. The Group of Seven territory. What Harris and the rest saw. The windswept trees. The bush that's never been tamed. The more I see of this place, the more I like it. I'm actually quite tired of the city, you know. The pollution and traffic and tons of people. I could live up here quite easily."

I remained quiet the rest of the drive back.

15

While I was at work, Lisa walked through the city with her camera, using up to two or three rolls of film a day. She wore her hiking boots, earth tone khakis, and black tops. She looked like a cultural Amazon ready to snap up any piece of unspoiled scenery or industrial wreckage the city had to offer.

"The light was good today," she said. "I went to the locks. Everything's in red sandstone."

"Some guys tried to follow me around," she said after another day of walking. "But they couldn't keep up with me."

In the evenings I drove her around. We saw a movie. Walked along the waterfront hand in hand. Visited the university library. Picked up the Toronto papers and had coffee at the Windsor. This is what life in the city would be like without children, I was tempted to tell her.

I took her to the tennis club, where I played tennis as she sat in the small bleachers reading Emily Carr.

"She's gorgeous," Paul Akropolis said to me at the net during a lull in play. Paul was a doctor whose left arm had been amputated for cancer while he was still in high school. He wore a prosthesis, was married with three young daughters, and played a good game of tennis and golf.

I looked at her with his eyes. She was undeniably striking, sitting there with her long legs and rounded figure. Her black attire, in the shade of the tall shrubbery behind her, gave her the appearance of a dark angel.

"What about that other girl, Janice?" he asked me.

Janice and I had played mixed doubles with him and his wife, Carrie.

"What about her?" I said.

The gap between my inner world and my outer world, however, skewered my vision. Instead of watching the ball, as Paul tossed it up with his racquet for the serve, I was watching what I thought was the ball. I lost six-love and six-two.

Later in the week we drove out to Kinsmen Park, known as Hiawatha Park when I was a kid. Only a few minutes on the highway and we were in the middle of the wilderness. It was hilly, with an old ski-jump, miles and miles of bush, and a winding stream and waterfalls. In the winter it was used as a cross-country ski area. A chalet rested at the top of the hill along the highway.

We trekked on the hilly trail along the stream for miles. The clean air and fresh pine smell were invigorating. We sat on a moss-covered ledge on a high ridge overlooking the bush.

The sun was low on our backs, the sky a deep blue.

"It's so beautiful here," Lisa said.

The bright sun cast long shadows over the forested valleys beneath us. The thick canopy of conifers and hardwoods was unbroken. It rolled as far as the eye could see. White pine, spruce, birch, poplar, maple, jackpine, as many varieties as there were hills.

I had forgotten how I used to enjoy going out into the bush when I was a kid. Walking over the humus. The rich odour of decaying leaves and trees and moss. Breaking the saplings. Canoeing over virgin creeks as clear as newly fallen rain. Lisa reminded me of my childhood friends. They all loved the sprawling wilderness, the solitude of the bush, the honesty and nakedness of the uncivilized heart.

"In Toronto you'd have to drive for at least an hour to get something like this," she added. "Here it's right in your back yard."

I nodded.

"But I'd still need New York," she said. "It'd just be two hours away, right? One hour to Toronto, and a connecting flight."

I nodded.

"D'you see how the light plays tricks with the colours of the trees?" she said. "It's so amazing. I can't find the words sometimes. And we can't even see it, you know. It's so ironic that light is invisible. Unless it's reflected and refracted."

I remained silent.

"That which makes everything else visible is itself invisible," she said. "Like consciousness."

I was listening, and yet thinking of something else.

"The Father of Lights," she said.

"Yes," I nodded.

"I've been studying light all my life, Croach. In ancient times the Egyptians thought of the sun as the eye of Ra. For the ancient Persians, the Zoroastrians, Ahura Mazda was the god of light. The creator God was opposed by Angra Mainyu or Ahriman, the God of Darkness. Then you have Lucifer, the bearer of light, and Prometheus, who stole fire from the gods, and Mani, the Envoy of Light, in Manichaeism. And Jesus, who's the Light of the World."

I looked at her. "You're an atheist."

"You can't personalize the light, Croach. The light is just the light."

"You just called it the Father of Lights."

"It's just an expression."

"The air is the breath of God," I said.

She shook her head. "In matters of religion, we're still children who after peeping into a mirror turn it around to see if God's on the other side."

I looked over the horizon of partially shaded, partially sun-drenched forest. The light was coming from the trees. But another light was coming from inside me, illuminating everything in meaningful expressions.

On Saturday morning, at five, we drove to the house under the bridge. My father was waiting for us. He had already packed the Ranger with food and equipment, had the outboard hooked up, and was having his coffee in the basement. In his green work pants and plaid cotton shirt, he appeared so happy I was embarrassed to look at him too long.

On the drive up the highway he mostly talked to Lisa, who sat in the back.

"It's a little early in the year for the fishing," he said, "so don't expect much. It's to get out and pass the time, that's only the one thing."

The highway became very hilly once we got past Batchewana. It curved along the Superior shore, showing us the expanse of Lake Superior and the wind-swept jack-pine that Lisa was looking for.

"It's simply beautiful up here," she said, her eyes like a wide open camera.

"Sometimes you forget that," my father said. "It's too close to you. Marco and me have been up here so much."

We passed the Montreal River and the power plant. I had been up here before to see the Indian pictographs. And then to hunt for moose.

We turned off the highway, deep into the bush, into an old logging road, and bumped along for miles, until the road abruptly ended at a shallow creek.

"This is it," my father said. "Help me get the boat in, Marco."

Once we had the supplies in the boat, we gingerly lowered it into the water, got in with our lifejackets on, and pushed off with the oars. It was too shallow for the motor at first. I did the honours while Lisa sat at the front, with her back to me. My father was at the back, keeping the motor tilted out of the water. The sun was higher in the sky now, and the light slanted through the tall birch, poplars, and conifers, down into the thick undergrowth of saplings and ferns. Birds were chirping everywhere. My father's eyes were focused into the thick forest as I slowly paddled along.

"Look, look!" he said, all excited. "Over there!"

I didn't see anything.

"I see it!" Lisa whispered.

"Where?" I said, pointing the oars out of the water.

Finally I saw it directly to our right. A small doe, its moist black nose perfectly still, sensing danger. It let the shadowy dapple-lighted forest hide it from sight.

Lisa looked as if she were exchanging signals with a long lost kindred spirit.

"It's just a deer," I said, resuming my paddling.

"It's out of season right now," my father said. "There aren't too many of those deer there left now. This place too is all hunted out. You have to go farther and farther north, by plane, like those big-shot Americans."

"You'd kill a deer, Nico?" Lisa said.

"No. But there're plenty of hunters who do. The Indians, they come down here and hunt too. That's how they

136

get some of their food. And they can get as much as they want, that's only the one thing."

"I don't believe in killing animals," Lisa said.

"But we're going fishing," I said.

"Oh, I'll throw them back if I catch any."

"You eat meat."

"Yes, I eat some meat. Yes, there's some inconsistency in my life. Yes, the big fish eats the little fish. Yes, nature is red in tooth and claw. But I'd rather be . . . something better than myself. As long as anything has life it has consciousness. It's part of me."

My father gave her a confused look.

"She's an artist, Dad. She'd rather paint animals than eat them."

When we got to deeper water, my father put the motor in and we quickly emerged into a large crystal clear lake, surrounded on all sides by the forested hills of the Cambrian Shield.

"My God!" Lisa swung her head around.

It was a spectacular sight as we motored out to the middle. No one else was in sight. No roads. No cottages. No antennae or planes.

I lowered the anchor in a small cove, not too far from a steeply-rising hill of Cambrian rock, and we set about baiting our hooks with juicy dew worms. The small waves slapped against the boat.

"Use a bob, Marco," my father said. "And cast out a bit from the boat."

From lowering the anchor I knew it was about ten feet to the bottom.

The first half-hour we focused on our bobs and lines. My father caught two fat perch and put them in the pail. Lisa caught a good-sized rock bass. She knew how to unhook the fish on her own with the pliers and threw it back in.

"Go ahead, fishy," she said. "Go back and do your fishy things."

Nico laughed. "I'll catch that same fish, Lisa, you'll see."

"No, no, Nico," she gave him her toothy grin. "I told that fish to eat no more worms today."

My bob went under and I felt a heavy pull on the line.

"It's Moby Dick!" I yelled out.

"Don't rock the boat," my father said calmly. "I'll get the net."

It turned out to be a three-pound lake trout.

"It's a beauty," my father held it up, smiling. "We'll eat it tonight."

Lisa made a face.

The fish stopped biting. We relaxed a bit. The sun rose higher. My father put on his straw hat. I gave Lisa a baseball cap. The sun was so dazzling off the water we couldn't look at it too long without our eyes watering. We heard far off noises. A rumbling truck somewhere in the hills. The sputter of a motor. Splashes. Birds. The call of the loon, sharp and clear over the water.

I tried to see the hills and forests like Lawren Harris. With simple intensity.

"I can give up Toronto for this any day," Lisa announced, sitting back on her seat, her cap low over her eyes.

"Would you live here in the sittee?" my father's voice got interested.

"Sure, I would."

"But there're no galleries here," I said. "No place to exhibit."

"How about this? Half a year here and half in Toronto."

My father was reading in between the lines like a bashful dog sniffing the air.

"I'd like to live in the big sittee too, you know," he said. "Berlin. Rome. Paris."

"Too bad you had to leave Italy, Nico. It's such a great place."

"Now it is maybe. But not during the war."

He told her about himself. How he had to leave school in grade five to work on his father's farm. How he envied everyone their schooling. The big shots, the *padroni*, who owned the sharecropper farms. How he learned to play the accordion to earn extra money and then went north to Germany before the war as a migrant worker. How he married Giulia Filippini just before the start of the war so that if anything happened to him she'd get the soldier's pension. How he was stationed in Yugoslavia to fight the partisans, then sent to a prisoner of war camp in Germany once the Mussolini government was deposed and Italy changed sides. How he made his way back to Pesaro after the war, in situations more life-risking than during, because of the presence of Russian soldiers in Germany. How he played the accordion in post-war Italy, with no money in his pockets, with no work anymore, when he saw the advertisement for the steel plant.

"It wasn't too hard for me to leave Italy," he said. "I had been away from home, to Germany and Yugoslavia. But it was hard on my wife, who had never travelled in her life outside Pesaro. Even now she has never learned English, hasn't learned to drive a car, and never wants to go on long trips out of the sittee."

We stared at him, the boat gently bobbing in the waves.

By mid-afternoon we'd had enough. We took in our lines. I lifted the anchor.

"So, Marco," my father said out of the blue, "isn't it about time you gave me a grandchild?"

The evening before Lisa was flying back to Toronto we were sitting out on the balcony after our meal and sipping coffee. I had my feet on the iron railing and was looking over the city. The sun was sinking over the steel plant as a red streaky ball.

"If only I could paint that colour," Lisa said. "Maybe Paris will do the trick. Aren't you looking forward to it?"

"A little. I'm more concerned about when the book comes out. I'll finally have justified all the years of failure."

Lisa swiped at the smoke from her cigarette.

"Listen, Croach," she said. "Either you give your notice here or, and this is a mighty *or*, or I come up and live here. I can't go through another year of separation."

"What about your degree?"

"I can do some teaching here and postpone the degree."

"You'd do that?"

"Of course," she eyed me. "But it makes more sense for you to find work in Toronto now. Then, if you want, we can come back here to live. I like it up here. The clean air. The open wilderness. The small-town atmosphere. I can trek for days in the bush. Maybe we could eventually get a cottage along Lake Superior."

I was pondering over this grand arrangement of my future when the doorbell rang, surprising the both of us.

"Were you expecting someone?" Lisa said.

I looked at her. I went to the door.

It was Janice standing there in the doorway, her eyes

popping out with a mixture of fear and anger. She was in jeans and a T-shirt that said *Life Sucks, Drink Juice*.

"Is she here?" she said, peering around me.

I glanced back towards the balcony where Lisa had an unobstructed view of us.

"I'd like to meet her," Janice looked past me to the balcony, where Lisa was already suspicious. "I'd like to see her with my own eyes. It's not enough that I have to imagine her and cause myself so much grief. I want to see how ordinary she is and put it all to rest. You've caused me so much heartache, you shit, I'd like to pay you back a bit."

By the time Lisa came up to us, I realized it was too late.

"Lisa James," I stepped aside, "this is Janice Harcourt."

They shook hands.

Lisa had seen everything in a flash. Janice's agitated state. Whatever guilt was on my face. And her experience with melodramas of this nature had undoubtedly filled in the rest.

"Won't you come in?" Lisa said. "Croach, get some coffee, please."

If I thought there was going to be some shouting, some hair pulling, or whatever, I was sadly mistaken. They were overly polite, sensitive to each other's pain, calm and proud. I, on the other hand, swallowed a lot that evening. Some saliva. More coffee. Some pride. A lot of silence. While they chatted and got to know each other.

Lisa asked Janice question after question. Janice's anger soon evaporated into open admiration. The only adversary left standing was me. Every so often they'd turn to me and smile the smile of a cagey reptile about to flick its tongue at an insect.

By the time Janice left I knew more about her than ever

before. I knew, for one, that I had hurt her more than she'd ever acknowledge. I knew that I had used her. I knew she'd never forgive me.

And then the fireworks started. Lisa and I didn't sleep at all that night.

16

Lisa went back to Toronto. She broke all contact with me. I had humiliated her beyond endurance, she said. I had deceived her for the last time. She didn't mind that much about a dalliance, as she called it, but I hadn't told her about it. That was the thing, she said. I hadn't told her.

"You take care of matters here with Janice," Lisa said at the airport, just before boarding the plane. "And we'll see about the Paris trip."

"Janice is history," I told her. "I won't see her again. It's you I want. I was just a little lonely up here, that's all."

"You take care of things," she said. "We'll see."

After she left, Janice, and I broke off. I spent some sorry time in the apartment bemoaning my fate.

Didn't I warn you? my godfather told me. The aesthetic stage is a hollow reed at the mercy of any wind. You need stability. A family. The ethical life. And then maybe you can take the leap.

But why did you take the ethical life? I asked him. Why didn't you marry and have a family?

I found a mission that I could live and die for, he said. To lead people to the authentic spiritual life. And I couldn't drag a woman I loved into my melancholia. Regine was vastly different. She'd soon tire of my earnestness.

Baloney, I told him. You didn't want your inner life compromised. You didn't want to give your real self to a woman. And you probably didn't have a strong sex drive.

Ingenlunde, he said in Danish. Not at all. I was in love.

You, on the other hand, love no one. You only need sex. You are fooling yourself. Your outer life is stronger than your inner life. Let's face the music, my friend. You and I are vastly different as well.

In late June, Lisa wrote about the Paris trip, asking me if we should still go. I had done everything possible to destroy our relationship, she wrote, but we still had Paris to contend with. Our plane tickets were unredeemable. We could try to sell them. The alternative was to go as friends. And at the end of the letter she had asked about Janice.

I phoned her immediately and told her I was no longer seeing Janice.

"I'm glad about Janice," she said. "It would be a shame to waste our tickets. We could go as friends. I've been thinking so much about us, Croach. I'm willing to give it one more chance. Are you?"

"Yes," I said.

"I can't give you up so easily," she said. "But by the end of the trip I need an answer from you. One way or the other. Is that clear?"

"Yes," I said.

Away from me she had become mythical again. I missed her. I wasn't sure about her. She was the woman who knew me through and through. There'd never be another like her. But she didn't want any kids. And I couldn't live on my nerve ends all the time. I needed solitude. I needed a hermetically sealed inner life that even my wife couldn't penetrate.

I didn't know what I wanted.

We met at the Toronto airport and boarded the plane for Paris. We were awkward with each other. And overly polite. A *Star Wars* movie was playing silently on the TV screens. Lisa was in her khaki slacks and sandals, her hair gleaming, her Amazonian body ready for combat or love.

"I'm so glad we're going," I said, my ears locked in the roar of the plane.

"It's up to you, Croach. You know how I feel. I've made it plain enough."

We chatted, catching up on lost news. She asked about Janice, wanting to know the little details.

"Are you sure about her?" she asked me.

"Yes, I'm sure."

Then monotony and fatigue brought back our old habits. She put her head on my shoulder and relaxed.

"Talk to me, Croach," she said. "Tell me why it's worth going to Paris."

I babbled on about this problem I was having. Of being a split being. Of growing up under the bridge with my secret inner life being my only consolation. My only means of survival. Of being nurtured by black blood and movies and dreams of escape.

"But I never could escape," I said. "Not really. You've seen my parents, Lisa. I haven't much changed from them, have I? I have a wider vocabulary, some knowledge of the wider world, but deep down they're who I am. On the outside. While you, you've made yourself into someone entirely different."

I told her how much I admired her. Her determination not to be mediocre. Her sense of purpose. Her artistic integrity.

"That's hooey, Croach. I'm no more than my parents, too. Believe me. I have the deepest fears. I don't drive. I can't cross the street without feeling anxious. Just like them. I'm meek and dependent, no matter what appearance I make."

"But you know who you are, Lisa. While me, I'm a great riddle to myself."

"You're not great, Croach. You're just a riddle," she smiled.

"I don't know what I really want."

"Well, I know what I want. I'm stupid in many ways, but I know what I want."

When we landed at Orly next morning, we saw the new French Concorde docked farther out on the tarmac. The sky was overcast. It was quite warm. We cashed a few traveller's cheques and took the airport express into the outskirts of the city. Then took a taxi.

"*Un hôtel bon marché*," Lisa instructed the driver. "*Sur la rive gauche. Nous sommes des étudiants.*"

He took the scenic route past the Eiffel Tower to the Left Bank, to a small hotel in the 5è arrondissement. Hôtel du Square Monge. Right in the thick of what was formerly the Sorbonne, close to St. Germain and La Rue Monge. The concierge took our passports. We had to pay for the whole week. Lisa gave me a look that said it was much too expensive.

The room was seedy-looking, with a saggy bed and a water-closet down the hall. The walls had faded wallpaper and tacky prints of Paris sights. We could hear the conversations next door. A faucet dripped in a sink behind a cloth partition.

"We made it," Lisa came into my arms and gave me a hug. "I'm so excited. Let's freshen up and go for a walk. The room's not great, but we're right in the Latin Quarter. We can start looking for a better place tomorrow."

I looked at the bed.

"Are we sleeping in the same bed?" I asked her.

"We'll take turns," she said. "I'll take the floor tonight."

"No, I'll take the floor."

"Don't be silly, Croach."

"I'm not being silly. I'll take the floor."

Later we went for a stroll to get our bearings. I started to get excited about being in Paris.

"When I was here before," Lisa said, "we stayed at a place close to Les Invalides and the Champs-de-Mars, not far from the Eiffel Tower, and I didn't like it at all. It was too close to the Military School. This is much better."

We walked past open air cafés and bookstores and restaurants and formidable-looking dark exteriors of schools that Lisa pointed out. École Polytechnique. Lycée Henri IV, where Sartre attended. Paris IV and the Sorbonne. L'École Normale Supérieure, attended by other intellectuals. We passed the Pantheon and found an inexpensive cafeteria on the Boule Miche. *Prix fixe*.

"Look!" Lisa pointed across the street. "A McDonald's!"

We liked cafeterias. No bother. No fuss. Just food on a tray. There'd be no fancy meals at the expensive restaurants for us. No going to the Lido and Crazy Horse nightclubs. No shopping at the couture houses with the designer clothes. Or even at Lafayette or La Samaritaine department stores. It wasn't exactly living on sardines like Mondrian, Lisa said, but we knew our priorities.

"I've been thinking about what you said on the plane," Lisa said, as she sipped on her espresso while fanning away the smoke from her Gauloise. "About you being a split being. And your godfathers. Like Kierkegaard."

"They give me direction. Purpose. A grander design to my paltry existence."

"Yeah, fine, okay," she nodded. "But you can't let them control your life. You have to be your own person, afterall."

I looked at her.

"I admire someone like Emily Carr," she went on. "But I don't let her control my life. I'm inspired by her passion for painting, her devotion to her work, her struggles to make it as a woman, but I'm not her. She was a lonely woman. I certainly don't want to end up like her. I don't want to end up with a miserable life just to be a good painter."

"I thought you'd sacrifice everything."

"Well," she said, shaking her head. "I can give up having a child. And having a comfortable life. But I need a man in my life. I couldn't be alone. But a man who can share everything with me. A man who's in control of his life."

I stared at her.

"You have to walk on your own two feet, Croach."

"Thanks."

"I'm serious. Look, let's just enjoy Paris, okay. Let's see what happens."

"Okay."

She took her Gauloise between her fingers like a Humphrey Bogart, her mouth curling around the cigarette with such sensuous enjoyment I was envious.

"It's a shame, Croach. A shame, you know. We'd be so good together. After that fishing trip with your father, I've often thought of us living in a little cottage up there. Close to the Superior shore. Away from McDonald's and TV and everything. Where you could do your work and I could do mine. Where we wouldn't need anyone else. We'd just have to take trips every so often. To New York and Paris. Get our fill of movies and galleries and books and then retreat back into seclusion."

I stared at her.

She took out *L'officiel des Spectacles*, which she had

picked up a corner kiosk, and quickly skimmed through the hundreds of movies playing in the city.

"Hey!" she pointed excitedly. "Here's a Jacques Tati Festival playing next week across the river. We should go and see it."

Her eyes panned the restaurant and glanced out the window. A stream of pedestrians passed by. She was excited about Paris, but a lingering sadness tightened her lips.

Later we strolled through the Luxembourg Gardens, where I saw statues of George Sand, Delacroix, Leconte de Lisle, and Sainte-Beuve. We sat on steel chairs facing the Grand Bassin on which children sailed boats. I saw tennis courts through the chestnut trees and felt a sudden pang of regret for not bringing my racquet.

"Tomorrow we'll go to the Louvre," Lisa said. "The next day to the Jeu de Paume, where the Impressionists are, and then to this new place, the Beaubourg, where there's a collection of modern art and a library open to the public. It's been built since my last trip. There's so much to see. Montmartre. Montparnasse. The Rodin Museum. La Place Pigalle, a red-light district. La Place de L'Opéra. Place de la Concorde. Notre Dame, of course. L'Hôtel des Invalides where Napoleon is buried. La Bibliothèque nationale."

Her excitement was infectious. But I felt I needed time to myself too. I needed to assimilate Paris on my own. Sometimes Lisa's very presence wore too thin. I was too attentive to her. She needed her solitude also, for her work, I knew. But I was working all the time – even when I wasn't at my desk. And I needed the silence to let the black blood percolate, bubble up to consciousness, explode into new connections and images.

And I needed to bang the tennis ball around too. Get some physical activity besides making love and walking.

The sun slowly sank over the trees in our first day in Paris. It was a little too hot to go back to our room, which had no air conditioner. So we strolled through the lighted cobblestone streets, smelled the coffee of the bistros and café-bars, and felt the Parisian air sink into our consciousness, until jet lag and fatigue got the better of us and we hurried back to our room.

She gave me the bed quilt and I slept on the floor on the little rug beside the bed.

The next morning I woke up with Lisa's hand in between my legs. She was stretched out beside me on the floor.

"Paris gets me so excited," she whispered in my ear. "Tell me you're really through with Janice."

17

The next few days we fell into a routine in visiting the art sites.

"We have to see this," Lisa said. "And this. And that."

My connection to Paris – and to ways French – was mainly through black blood. I had taken some French in university. *L'Étranger. Le Grand Meaulnes. Madame Bovary. La Nausée.* But most of what I had read was in translation. Such as *Remembrances of Things Past* in the small blue-bound volumes in my hometown library, which I had gone through at least three times. It wasn't so much the Proustian sensibility and content, which were entirely foreign to me, or the endless references to his pseudonymous characters much like Kierkegaard's. It was the oceanic flow of language, the grand house of words he had fashioned. Nothing touched me more than Proust's deathbed picture by Man Ray with the piles of manuscript beside his corpse in his cork-lined room. No matter what a reprobate he was in life, in death he looked like a saint. He had spent the latter part of his life pouring his black blood onto those pages. I saw his emaciated body on the bed. I saw his blood still beating in those manuscript pages.

And Honoré Balzac drinking his coffee night after night. To stave off his creditors. Creating those two tomes of another grand oeuvre of arteries and veins of black blood that I had picked up in the library my first year of university.

These were the lives worthy of emulation for a kid from the north. Lisa was right, of course. I had to stand on my own two feet. Quit using these people as substitute fathers.

But in making myself a new being I had drunk the blood of worthy teachers. And like Plato, I believed that we were who we were before we were born. It was just a matter of spending our lives recollecting our visions.

For me, Paris was the home of the existentialists and Marxists. The *nouveau roman* and the new wave in the cinema. The expats like Beckett and Joyce and Hemingway. The French respected black blood. The classical prose of Descartes and Pascal and Madame de Sévigné was still emulated by French schoolboys.

For Lisa, of course, Paris was the former art centre of the world.

We spent two days in the Louvre.

For people who came to Paris regularly certain sights were commonplace. For me, however, I was seeing things with the eyes of one who had been raised in a cave.

The large Delacroix, David, and Géricault canvases in La Grande Gallerie wing flooded my eyes. I was blinded by the large statue at the head of the stairs. The Victory of Samothrace. A huge headless winged woman mounted on blocks of stone. It looked like the prow of a ship and dated back to 200 BC. Her wings were immense. Her headless torso pushed forward against all odds.

"That's you," I said to Lisa.

She laughed, flattered. "My thighs aren't *that* large."

Certainly she was more akin to The Victory than to the Venus di Milo, which was dainty and docile, with a beauty reserved more for court concubines and maidservants.

Another day we spent an afternoon at the Jeu de

Paume, a pavilion at the head of the Tuilleries Gardens, abutting the Place de la Concorde. Most of the French Impressionists were temporarily sequestered here. Lisa took me from room to room, from Van Gogh to Monet, Manet to Renoir, from Pissarro to Sisley, Dégas to Cézanne.

"These are the ones most interested in light," she told me. "The fleeting unstable effects of light. Maybe like your moments of being."

Outside, on steel chairs, at La Place de la Concorde, we ate a lunch of bread and cheese. The sight lines were brilliant. To the east were the Tuilleries Gardens and Louvre. To the west, on a slow rise on the Champs-Élysée was the L'Arc de Triomphe. To the south, across the Concorde bridge over the Seine, was the National Assembly. And over to the north, up the Rue Royal, was the façade of la Madeleine church.

"This is where thousands of heads rolled off the guillotine in the 1790s," Lisa told me, looking at the Obelisk, as the endless traffic circled the large square.

We eased into the flow of Paris routine. When to have an espresso at the nearest café-bar. When stores closed and re-opened. When to eat. When the *International Herald Tribune* was available at the nearest kiosk. The difference between *Le Monde* and *Le Figaro*. The location of the movie theatres in the area. The cheaper restaurants. Where to buy the best baguettes. The routes of the Metro, which was the cheapest and fastest form of travel.

But our efforts to find another cheaper place were unsuccessful.

"We'll have to look for a sublet," Lisa said. "The Parisians are starting to leave for *les vacances*. It'll be cheaper in the long run. We can cook our own meals. Otherwise we won't be able to last much longer."

We spent most of the days walking and building up our appetites. Up the many flights of stairs to Montmartre, to Sacré-Coeur and the cemetery. On the gravestones were names that stirred my blood. Zola and Heine. Dumas and Renan. Dégas and Stendhal.

"You love these cemeteries, don't you?" Lisa said.

"I've always tried to establish contact with the dead," I said.

"We'll go and see Père Lachaise then. And La Maison Balzac. You're the reverse vampire, aren't you? You suck dead blood."

We walked along the quais of the Seine, where *les bouquinists* had their endless stalls of postcards and sketches and paperbacks. Sometimes Lisa had more energy than me. She could walk miles, in her long loping strides, as if she had invisible wings. When I would suggest the subway home, she'd look incredulously at me.

"But you can't see anything from the Metro," she'd say.

"The bus then."

We went to Shakespeare & Co., the former Sylvia Beech bookstore, no longer on the rue de l'Odéon. It was now close to the Seine, on the left bank, not far from Notre Dame. It was musty inside, with old sofas and reading chairs and plenty of used books, mostly in English. I found a good copy of *Being and Time*, Heidegger's masterpiece, and remembered Karl Scheler's advice. Lisa bought a biography of Cézanne and a collection of essays by Roger Fry.

We walked up the Champs-Élysée towards the Arc de Triomphe, past all the airline offices, banks, and embassies, past the fashionable and expensive cafés that we'd never frequent.

Then we doubled back to the Trocadéro and climbed

the incline of the Palais Chaillot to face the Eiffel Tower.

By the time we got back to the hotel, after stopping for our only good meal of the day, we were usually too exhausted to make love. Or it was so hot and humid we preferred to catch a cheap double-bill in one of the air-conditioned theatres around the Sorbonne. According to the *L'Officiel des Spectacles*, every conceivable film was playing in the city. We could see festivals devoted to Humphrey Bogart, Jacques Tati, Ingmar Bergman, Laurel and Hardy, Claude Chabrol, and others. There were Italian costume epics going back to the fifties, classic French films like *Le Grand Illusion*, one of my favourites, along with *Les Enfants du Paradis*, Swedish films, and Brazilian films like *Xica da Silva*. There were dubbed films like *La Fièvre du Samedi Soir* and *La Guerre des Étoiles*, which we saw on the plane. And rock films like *The Doors*, *Jimi Plays Berkeley* and *Let It Be* and *Pink Floyd*. Porn films like *Positions Danoises*, which would surely make Kierkegaard turn in his grave, and *Lolita Prête à Tout*. *Citizen Kane* was playing, as well as *Le Dernier Tango à Paris* and *L'Année Dernière à Marienbad*, *L'Énigme de Kaspar Hauser* and *Aguirre la Colère de Dieu*.

Paris was movies, bookstores, cafés, and the unchanged splendour of the boulevards and 19th century buildings of Haussmann.

As if reading my mind, Lisa said, "I could definitely live here, couldn't you?"

If she had her way – and the money, to boot – she'd live in New York, Paris, the Soo, and the Island of Dr. Moreau. She'd be a citizen of the world.

Every morning we went out for breakfast to the corner bar-café. I liked the smell of espresso mixed with Gauloise and Gitane smoke, and the fresh editions of *Le Monde*. I liked buying a new French book, cutting the pages open and inhaling the full aroma of the virgin-published pages.

It occurred to me that Kierkegaard wouldn't have been so ironic if he had lived in Paris.

But maybe he'd rail at French intellectual atheism, not to mention French decadence in regard to sex. Maybe only a France could've produced a Marquis de Sade, it occurred to me, after I saw, alone, a French porn flic where a man urinated on a woman before screwing her from behind.

The live sex shows were amply advertised.

One night, after seeing a Marx Brothers double-feature at an air-conditioned theatre up the street from the Hôtel Monge, Lisa and I had a big fight.

It started with a small matter, really, when she objected to my sneaking off to see that one porn film. But as we were walking back to our hotel room, things got out of hand.

"I'm just saying you should've told me," she said. "I don't want to have to see a ticket stub to find out."

"Why do I have to tell you everything?" I protested.

"Don't be sneaky, Croach," she looked away, as we walked down the cobblestone streets, her head held high. "It's beneath you."

"I'm not being sneaky. I just have to do things on my own."

"That's what I'm saying," she made her voice hard. "Only tell me about them. Not like Janice. And Bella Nardi."

"If I tell you about them, then they're not entirely my own, are they?"

She stared at me, flabbergasted at this Trecroci bit of logic.

"Look, Croach, if we're to get back together, we have to be entirely open. I don't want to have to go through what I've gone through. Okay?"

I paused and chose my words carefully. "I've got to do a lot on my own."

"Of course," she said. "That's not my point. But you should let me know what you're doing. And whom you're doing it with. I deserve to know everything."

"Everything?" I said.

"Everything that concerns us."

That night, as we were making love in bed, I put my fingers inside her and then brought them up to my nose. Instead of exciting me, as it usually did, her sex smell had the opposite effect.

"Lisa, I have to tell you something," I said.

It was quiet on the *troisième étage*. Everyone was in bed. It was past midnight. The air was stifling. The window was open and we were naked without any sheets over us.

The gravity in my voice let her know something was up. She was ready to continue our relationship, I knew, but I had to put a stop to it, whether it would ruin the rest of our trip or not. Tonight's little chiding of me had turned the screws too tight.

"What is it?" she said.

"I can't pretend anymore," I said.

She stared at me without blinking.

"What do you mean?" she said. "What're you saying?"

"It's no use. I can't pretend."

"What?"

I paused, knowing what I would say next would open the floodgates.

"I just can't pretend," I said.

"About what?"

157

"I don't love you," I said.

She froze. "You love someone else?"

"No."

"You're still with Janice."

"No."

We lay side by side. Time passed. Then she took my hand and put it around her shoulders and tried to get me to continue making love. But I couldn't. I was frozen. I was limp.

"Please, Croach," she whimpered. "Don't be like that, please."

"I mean it. It's no use, Lisa."

She began to sob in a desperate way, moving my hands about as if trying to get a corpse to make love to her. She kissed my face. I felt her hot tears. Drool came out of her mouth.

"Please, Croach, don't scare me like this . . ."

I lay immobile and limp, the life all out of me. Everything she was doing made things worse. I couldn't respond.

"Don't scare me, please . . . "

"Stop it!" I finally shouted, pushing her away.

She recoiled from me as if I had struck her. She shrank into a foetal ball and emitted a ghastly whimper.

I sat up in bed, my back to her.

She made inhuman sounds. Loud groans, followed by soft mewling puffs of air, such as a hurt animal might make caught in a bear trap. It made me feel like a total ogre. But it was all beyond me. I knew I couldn't go on with her. It was physically impossible.

This went on a while. Then she stopped.

"Why did you have to drag me all the way to Paris to tell me?" she said.

"I don't know," I said. "I guess I didn't know at the time."

"It's so cruel. I could never believe you were so cruel."

"Please, Lisa. Please."

"I've never met a guy so cruel as you, Croach," she said. "This can't be happening. How can you destroy something that was so good? I just can't believe it. Croach? Speak to me."

I was silent.

Later she tried to kiss me. "I don't care if you don't love me. Please make love to me," she pleaded. "Please. Make the pain go away. Please."

Drool was coming out of her mouth. She had become a hideous caricature of herself. Her nakedness began to repel me. Her dark eyes were coated in dirty water.

I couldn't respond. It was about two o'clock. My body was drenched in sweat. Sleep pulled my eyelids down. I was nodding off.

She tried again. Nothing worked. She sobbed some more, then stopped and lay quiet, her back against me. It was silent for a long while.

She took the wet bedsheet and a pillow and lay down on the floor beside the bed.

"What're you doing?" I said.

"What does it look like?" she said, curling her body into a foetal position into the wet sheet even though it was stifling in the room.

"Don't be ridiculous," I raised my voice. "Come back to bed."

"No."

She was being childish. I pleaded with her to come back to bed.

"I'll pick you up and put you on the bed," I said.

Her head flashed out of the comforter.

"Don't you dare touch me!"

I pleaded with her to switch places with me and she didn't want to do that either.

Finally, my eyelids felt so droopy that it didn't matter anymore who was sleeping where.

"I found us a sublet on the rue St. Jacques," I heard her say in a flat voice. "Just south of here. We have to go and be interviewed tomorrow."

18

The next day, when the hot sun came through the Venetian blinds, we woke up as strangers.

As we were going to the interview we agreed to pretend that everything was all right. We couldn't afford separate rooms. And we needed more space.

The new place was much larger and more modern. It had air conditioning in a good building, was two flights up with an elevator, and was filled with books. Mme Gdalia, the owner, was a thin middle-aged journalist. She was off to north Africa on a vacation/assignment deal and was able to sublet to us for as long as four weeks at a good rate. We had to water the plants and take care of her cats. We also had to give her a hefty down payment in case of damage. She liked the fact that Lisa was a graduate student, an artist, and that we seemed "simpatici." She didn't ask about our relationship, but she did have our passports checked and everything was in order.

She left carefully written instructions on how to feed the cats and water the plants.

We moved in the next day. The apartment made a world of difference. Not only the air conditioning, but the three separate rooms and the bathroom gave us space to manoeuvre and have privacy. I enjoyed the books and the unpretentious comfortable furniture, especially the reading chairs. We were closer to the Luxembourg Gardens, only a few blocks from the Boule Miche and close to the rue Gay Lussac. Fruit stores, boulangeries, and grocery stores with everything we needed, including cheap wine, were within easy reach.

Lisa was aloof and business-like. When I looked at her, she turned away.

Later in the evening she celebrated our good fortune by making a large fancy omelet, with tons of vegetables.

We ate quietly at the kitchen table. A counter jutted out beside the gas stove and fridge. Mme Gdalia had put everything at our disposal. I observed Lisa's drawn face, the lines on her forehead, the way she avoided my eyes.

It was as if someone had changed the lens through which I perceived her.

We talked inanities. I told her I planned to buy a racquet and play some tennis at the Luxembourg. She said she was going to the Beaubourg tomorrow and if I'd like to come along.

I nodded. "Where is it?"

"On the other side of the river. Where Les Halles used to be. Just north of Notre Dame and L'Hôtel de Ville."

Our usual procedure to break in a new apartment or room was to make love. As we consumed a little more wine than usual I knew it was coming – and I became anxious.

All I wanted to do was go out alone and walk the streets. The proximity to her was suffocating.

"Croach, we have to talk," she said, taking her glass of wine.

We went to the living room and sat on the beige wicker sofa that had too many cushions. The cats were between us, true owners of the place. There was a glass coffee table and a magazine rack. I saw *Paris Match*. *Elle*. And *L'Humanité*, the Communist newspaper. The window with the Venetian blinds looked over the rue St. Jacques. Over the roofs I could see some of the trees of the Luxembourg.

"Croach, I think we should sleep in separate beds for a while," she announced. "Until we get this problem solved."

I nodded.

She gave me a sorrowful look. "What happened, Croach?"

"I don't know," I said. "I've just reached a point where I can't pretend anymore. My body won't let me. You said this trip would make the difference. It has."

She looked at me as if she couldn't believe my words.

"Were you ever in love with me?" she said.

"I don't know. I guess I was. I admire you so much. I respect you. You've been my good friend. You've taught me so much about art. And you're so much more noble and devoted than me. But I don't know. It's like my body's rebelling or something."

"What a slimy piece of shit you are," she said.

I looked at her.

"How could you put me through this?" she said.

"Believe me, I didn't know till the other night. It just hit me. Please don't start."

Her face seemed lost. She choked back the tears.

That night I took the sofa, displacing the cats, who were none too pleased. Lisa took Mme Gdalia's queen size bed.

The next morning I woke up early and went out for a café au lait at a bar-café down the street. Sweepers in blue smocks were cleaning the sidewalks as the water gushed down the gutters of the cobblestone street. It was cool that early and the sun was shining. I was in a strange mood. Heavy-hearted, yet light-headed. I walked the short distance to the Luxembourg Gardens and sat in a steel chair close to the tennis courts.

I had the Heidegger book with me. The air was fresh and invigorating. I got to the fifth page before I realized I couldn't move on to a new godfather until I made peace with the old one.

Why didn't you marry the woman you loved? I asked Kierkegaard.

I couldn't marry her in the outer world, he said, and lead a worldly life. It wouldn't have worked at all.

I think I need the safe worldly life, I said.

What about the leap? he said. The hemlock or the cross?

Black blood will be my hemlock, I said.

Lost in my reveries, I didn't realize two young ladies had sat close by in tennis whites to wait for a court.

They were both quite attractive. The one closest to me was very tall and slim, with brown hair tied severely back in a pony tail and the sharp features of a fashion model. The other, much shorter, was fair-haired, with a cupid lips and the body of an athlete. They both had quality racquets sticking out of their bags and looked like serious players.

"*Mira*," the shorter one said, "*j'ai le cafard ce matin*."

"*Mais oui, c'est dommage*."

"*C'est possible?*"

"*Oui, c'est possible*," the tall one said, and then spoke in an English without any accent. "We'll have to find other tennis partners, that's all. Better than them. Afterall, they weren't that good, you know."

When a court became available, they sauntered on and bashed the ball with expert ground strokes. I watched carefully as they glided over the chalky clay surface behind the mesh partition, sometimes hitting the ball so hard they grunted through their strokes. The tall one had classic strokes, a two-handed backhand, and a wicked forehand that looped the ball just inches above the net. The short one took the ball early on the bounce and put underspin deep into the backcourt. Most of the other players were hackers. A few were watching the young ladies at the corner of their eyes.

A flock of pigeons fluttered down close to my feet, bobbing their heads and cooing, as if waiting for a handout.

As the sun came over the trees, it hit the chalky surface of the courts and dazzled my eyes.

Though I was totally blind to many things in the world, there were moments like this when I saw clearly.

Lisa had taught me to see the light and the dark. But the path I had chosen was only for two feet, and not even real feet at that. It was a journey without feet, as Plotinus said.

When the girls came off, their skin was lathered with sweat. They sauntered over like queens of the Luxembourg. I stared at their loveliness, their glowing and ripe health, their skill and power, their force that through their sex drove the world.

"*Vous êtes formidables*," I blurted out with open admiration.

"*Va te faire foutre!*" the shorter one barked at me, entirely pissed off.

"Who're you?" the tall one said, coming up to my chair.

I stood and introduced myself. She looked at the black Heidegger book. I explained that I'd be more than a match for them in tennis. But I hadn't brought my racquet, I said. If they'd be so kind as to lend me one of theirs tomorrow morning, I'd show them a thing or two.

"Oh, yeah?" she said, picking up the book. "You read Heedigger, eh? Where're you from? Your accent sounds familiar."

She stood even with me and looked me in the eye.

I told her. "I'm staying at the rue St. Jacques just over there around the corner. For another three weeks. I can give you a good game, believe me."

"You're Canadian, uh," she laughed. *"As-tu écoutée, Delphine? C'est un canadien."*

The short one shrugged.

The tall one introduced herself as Mira Lackovic, from Montreal, originally from Yugoslavia, a Croat. She was in Paris visiting her friend Delphine here, who used to live in Montreal as well.

Then, before they left, she threw out a challenge.

"You be here tomorrow at nine o'clock and we'll see how good you are."

When I got back, Lisa was reading. She asked me where I had been. I told her the Luxembourg, reading and watching tennis.

After lunch we walked down the rue St. Jacques, across the Seine and the Île de la Cité and up rue St. Martin, turned right, and came upon the Beaubourg, set back from a large cobblestone square.

I'd never seen such a building. It was five storeys high, made of glass and steel rods that made it look like it was encrusted with scaffolding. There were pipes, ventilator shafts painted red, blue, green, and yellow, and glass tubular escalators on the outside that looked like giant caterpillars. In the square various groupings of spectators were watching acrobats, jugglers, fire-eaters, and other street performers.

We immediately went to the National Museum of Modern Art where we paid a modest sum to enter. Lisa acted very distant. She went off on her own, leaving me to observe alone. I hurried through the Légers and Utrillos, passed Picasso, Kandinsky, and Modigliani, saw the Matisse and Delaunay. The one piece that arrested my attention was *The Snake Charmer* by Rousseau. It was dark and green and primitively mysterious in the open light of the glassy building.

But a heavy torpor overcame me. All the colour and light of the artworks had glutted my eyes. It was too much. I longed for darkness. For silence. I longed for the inward life into the cave rather than out into the light. My journey without feet.

I told Lisa I couldn't take any more art. I'd wait for her in the English library on another floor.

I felt I was in a hothouse, my blood being pounded by the bright colours of a foreign sensibility.

One section of the library was devoted to audio-visual material. A group of people with headphones were watching Sartre being interviewed on a TV screen. Then, while browsing through the stacks, I came upon an interesting book that explained Heidegger's thought.

By the time Lisa came round, about two hours later, I was in a high state of excitement. I had stumbled on the key to Heidegger's world. His new-fangled ontological terms weren't as daunting. I began to see what he meant. By Dasein. Being-in-the-world. The ontic. Attunement. *Sorge*. By fallenness. By falling captive to the world. By dis-owning oneself. By *Das-man*, the "them." By his mystical regard for language.

It was a lot of Kierkegaard explained in secular fashion.

We took the metro back. Lisa wanted to eat out. We found a place with reasonable rates on the Rue Gay Lussac. It reminded me of the Blue Cellar Room – a cave-like interior, with red-checked table cloths and peasanty decor.

When our bottle of wine arrived, I told Lisa about my excitement over Heidegger. I'd have to go back to the Beaubourg often, I said, since the books weren't for circulation.

She took the news with a blank face.

"How can you be in such a good mood?" she said. "I can't sleep at night. I can hardly keep down my food."

"Lisa . . ." I shook my head.

"How did you become such a shit?"

I stayed quiet.

"Okay, listen," she said a little later, some cheeriness coming back to her voice. "Let's have a good meal, drink a lot of wine, go back to the apartment, and see what happens. If we don't get along, this trip will be a nightmare."

I didn't object. I'd agree to anything to get us out of this heavy pall that hung over us. She lost her downcast expression and talked about the artwork at the Beaubourg. The meal was delicious, and the wine lubricated our spirits. I looked forward to easing some of the terrible tension between us.

We got to the apartment. Lisa was very tipsy. She didn't waste any time, coming into my arms and kissing me.

"You've been so bad," she hissed in my ear. "Such a bad boy. You've caused me so much heartache. You go right into Mme Gdalia's bed and wait for me. I have to go to the bathroom first."

I went to the bedroom and slipped into bed naked. I was on tenterhooks, not sure I could go through with it. Everything had changed between us. I couldn't completely fathom what had happened.

Lisa came back and sat on the bed. The wine had made her amorous. She took off her clothes and cuddled up to me.

I felt her warm skin and smelled her hair. I felt her breasts push into me. She was hungry with desire, but tentative as well, unsure of my response.

I went through the motions. She grinded herself into me, her desire open. I became aroused. I put my nose into her neck. I could smell a faint odour of paint. I dipped my face down and took her nipple into my mouth. She moaned. She pushed my head down farther. She was writhing with excitement. I inhaled deeply and smelled her strong sex odour. Again it stopped me in my tracks and kicked the desire out of me.

I froze.

"What's the matter?" she said.

I couldn't speak. I couldn't move.

"I can't, Lisa."

"Not again!"

We remained silent. With each passing second I could feel her frustration mounting.

"I just can't go on," I told her.

"Please," she begged, pressing against me.

I remained frozen, my cock totally limp.

She went berserk. Absolutely stark raving mad. She pounded her fists against my chest. She cursed me. I didn't fight back.

Her face was soaked in tears, mucous dribbling down her chin.

I was shocked deeper into silence. She could've been a heart-broken mother blaming me for killing her child.

"I despise you!" she screamed at me. "I despise you so much I can't bear to be in the same room with you!"

With that, she grabbed the comforter and dashed out of the bedroom.

I heard her knocking things down. One of the cats

squealed in pain. Then she seemed to settle down on the sofa. And finally some silence.

I tried to sleep. Every so often I heard sobs, heart-rending sobs that shook me up.

During the night I remembered being half asleep. I opened my eyes and groggily deciphered a shape standing above me. It was a naked woman with long flowing hair and a snake coiling around her neck. She had an instrument in her hand. It was either a reed pipe or a knife. I couldn't make it out. I was too groggy with sleep to react. I knew she wanted to stab me, not to charm me. I knew I had betrayed her beyond belief. But I couldn't help it. My body had spoken.

As I groggily fluttered my eyes, I saw the kitchen knife poised above my chest.

"No, Lisa, no," I remembered my lips forming the silent words in the still room of the foreign apartment.

The next morning, when I went to the bathroom, I saw that Lisa had left. There was a note on the coffee table beside the sofa.

I can't have you speak to me anymore. We will try to get through this terrible time as best we can. I will be gone each morning for most of the day. Please try not to be in the apartment from six to ten each evening. I will try to get an early flight out of Paris as soon as I can. You can have the apartment to yourself if I do leave.

I dragged myself to the Luxembourg Gardens and the tennis courts. My energy exploded on the court. I had a good hit with Mira, who was impressed with my play.

"You're pretty good," she said afterwards, towelling her face. "Have you got a friend for Delphine?"

"No, there's just me."

"Do you want to play again?"

"Sure," I said, handing her back the racquet.

"Okay, every morning at ten o'clock."

19

In the next week I fell into a routine.

True to her word, Lisa was gone every day by the time I awoke. The apartment was warm and comfortable in the early morning. I fetched *Le Figaro* at the nearest kiosk, had my coffee and toast, and read for an hour or so.

Then it was off to the tennis courts to bash the ball around with Mira Lackovic. Followed by a quick shower and my walk to the Beaubourg. I sat at the same desk every day and read Heidegger or about Heidegger. Kierkegaard's voice became fainter and fainter in my mind. I went for long walks. To the Bois de Vincennes, the Bois de Boulogne. The Place de la République. Crisscrossing the streets endlessly, getting to know it from all angles. After a late meal I finished the day by going to a movie or watching some TV.

Every so often I varied the routine.

One day I spent the afternoon at the Père Lachaise cemetery. It was spread out over a wide hilly area of trees and winding paths. The above-ground crypts were large enough for vagrants to sleep in. Tucked away in a corner was the burial place of Heloise and Abelard, with overgrown shrubbery around it. *Douzième siècle*, the inscription said, though it had been there for only two hundred years, donated by an admiring duchess or other. The statues of the noted lovers were reclining under a canopy, united for eternity.

As I strolled over the worn paths with a small map, I

caught the noted politicians, painters, writers, and celebrities. Some like Oscar Wilde and Jim Morrison had large monuments, newly honoured or desecrated. Some, like Delacroix, had simple slabs long neglected. I felt honoured to be in the dead presence of Proust and Victor Hugo, Molière and Balzac.

Another day I went to the Maison de Balzac in a residential district in Passy near the Bois de Boulogne.

I walked gingerly inside the small country house preserved in the style of the 1840s. It had low ceilings and tiny rooms. Balzac's famous Limoges coffee maker rested on his writing desk. Complete editions of *La Comédie Humaine* were inside glass bookcases. In the back was a small garden of trees and shrubbery on the edge of a hill. I sat on a bench and tried to imagine my dead godfather sitting on the same bench over a century ago. Then I remembered his dauntless sculpture that Lisa and I had seen at MoMa.

Live it forwards, understand it backwards, said Kierkegaard.

Mira Lackovic advised me to see Napoleon's tomb at Les Invalides and the Rodin Museum.

"They're both splendid," she said.

One time I strolled through the rue St. Denis, with its street walkers in colourful garb, and through La Place Pigalle where the lights of the Moulin Rouge lit up the shapes of women lurking in the entrances and alleyways like a B-movie.

At night I slept in Mme Gdalia's bed in dire guilt while Lisa was in the living room on the sofa. I left the bed lamp on, in case I had to ward off her blows. I had written her notes suggesting a switch of sleeping arrangements, but I found each one crumpled up in answer. It was as if she was punishing me by sacrificing her comfort.

I thought she'd ease up a bit by the end of the week. But it didn't happen. She wouldn't speak to me.

Some nights my eyes fluttered open and I heard faint sobs from the living room. They sounded inhuman, ghastly, as if I had ripped her heart open.

Sometimes I woke up in the middle of the night in a panic, half expecting her to be hovering over me with a knife in her hand. Like Clytemnestra in Central Park, murderess of her own husband, Destiny's Minister of blood. When I took a shower I left the curtain partially open.

It was impossible for us not to bump into each other occasionally. When we did, usually at the door or on the way to the bathroom, she'd fix me such Medusa looks that I had to avert my eyes.

I remembered my two-year feud with my sister, when we didn't speak a word to each other. At the beginning, every look had hardened our hearts a little more, until after a few months it was impossible to make up.

I only had a vague idea of what she did during the day. Probably a lot of time at the Louvre and other museums and galleries, especially those days when the entrance was free. She didn't have much money left. And the early flight hadn't materialized, according to a note she left me. She couldn't afford it, she wrote. And she reminded me to clean up after myself in the kitchen.

Towards the middle of the second week Mira and I met for dinner at my favourite cafeteria on the Boule Miche.

"Delphine and I come here every so often," Mira said. "Though it gets too touristy at this time of the year."

Outside the front windows I noticed a Spectacle Column with its ubiquitous ads for The Crazy Horse and Le

Moulin Rouge. Underneath were smaller ads for museum and gallery exhibits. *Exposition d'Oeuvres de Peintures Soviétiques. Oeuvres de Matisse à Warhol. Georges Rouault.*

Mira's height and figure easily turned men's heads. She wore short skirts that showed miles of leg. She pinned her hair up like a sassy courtesan. Her moist face gleamed at attention. I called her The Tall One. She put a lot of top-spin on the ball. She drove it deep into the backcourt.

She told me about the two guys who had ditched her and Delphine. The young men told them they were two junior execs from Boston on a business trip. They played a good game of tennis and had money to burn.

"One time," she said, her eyes fluttering around the cafeteria, "they took us to the Moulin Rouge, all hoity-toity, and then, in the car, opened a briefcase with a gun in it. Del and I almost peed our pants. No one said a word about it, but we definitely got the impression they were shady characters and not to be trifled with."

I smiled. "You like dangerous guys, Mira?"

She looked me in the eye. "I like *interesting* guys. For example, what you were reading at the courts the first time we met. Heedigger. That's interesting. I've always wanted to know more about these guys. Because these nose-high intellectuals around here are always talking about Hegel and Marx, like they're two long lost brothers or something, you know."

I corrected her pronunciation on Heedigger. She blushed and immediately got her dander up.

"You think I'm stupid, uh?"

"Not in the least," I cooly said. "I think you play a great game of tennis, look fantastic without designer clothes, and are as sharp as a tack in spotting interesting guys."

"Are you making fun of me?" she gave me a suspicious glance.

"Definitely. And you're allowed to make fun of me as much as you want as well."

Without blinking she said, "Your backhand needs a little work. And who says you're allowing me?"

I laughed. "Point well taken."

After she'd eaten her *filet de boeuf au poivre*, she excused herself and came back with her face cleared of makeup. It looked fresh and wonderful. And I liked her for that. Mira had a veil of sassy outspokenness on the outside. And underneath a little girl's charm and uncertainty.

She told me about herself, how she left Split in Croatia when she was twenty, settled in Montreal with her parents, did modelling work, and now was doing amateur theatre and part-time teaching.

"Did I tell you I won the Miss Split pageant," she said. "Every so often I had to do farm festivals. Exhibits. Luncheons with sports celebrities."

I reared back in mock surprise and made a slight bow. "I feel honoured to even know you."

"You should be," she lifted her head like a duchess. "And I feel totally insulted you didn't ask me out sooner. You must have a girlfriend somewhere and be entirely under her thumb."

I laughed. "Yes, that's exactly it. Would you like to meet her?"

It was her turn to be surprised.

I told her about Lisa, our breakup, and the pickle we were presently in.

"You told us you lived alone," she shook her finger at me.

"For all intents and purposes, I do," I said. "We hardly see each other. We leave notes. She hates my guts. It's over. But we can't afford to get separate places."

"I don't want any part of that," she said, looking away in annoyance. "She sounds dangerous. And, besides, you're leaving in a week or so."

"Montreal and Toronto aren't that far apart," I said. "And I can always help you find a permanent teaching job if you want."

A few nights later we went to a movie. *En route pour la gloire. Bound for Glory*, it said at the bottom of the marquee. The story of Woody Guthrie. Afterwards we strolled through the Latin Quarter. It was a mild night. We walked along the Seine to the Pont Neuf and sat on one of the circular stone benches. The river gleamed with points of light. Behind us loomed the bulk of Notre Dame. Across the river was the Samaritaine and the Louvre. Cars streamed by.

"Delphine's mad at me," Mira said. "I'm visiting her and I'm going out with you."

"How about a ménage à trois?"

"You'd like that, wouldn't you?"

"I don't think I can handle you alone, Miss Split, let alone with another girl. And that's the truth."

"That's damn right, my friend. You'd be hard pressed to handle me alone."

"I don't disagree," I reared back. "But I have Heedigger to guide me."

She laughed. "You're a joker. But you know what? I always dreamed of being in Paris with a guy I liked."

I felt touched by her words, even if they were pretense. She was looking at the river. The points of light bounced off her face. But she was too substantial to be a mere impression of light. She had as much substance as the looming presence of the church farther down the river.

"Look at this river," she said, awe in her voice. "Just look at it."

"I'm looking," I said, regarding her profile. What had I done to deserve such luck?

I took her hand and we walked back towards the St. Germain-des-près area where Delphine had her apartment.

A couple of evenings later we met for coffee close to the rue St. Jacques and I invited her up to Mme Gdalia's apartment.

"I don't think so," Mira said.

"Lisa's gone to Versailles for the whole day. It'll be all right, believe me."

"Who's the owner?" she said, when I ushered her in. She walked right by the shelves of books. "This is quite the place."

"A journalist." I told her about Mme Gdalia, whose presence had been effaced from the apartment. She had shelved any photos and personal nicknacks. Only the cats, who had voracious appetites and seemed always in the way, were visible reminders of the owner.

We sipped wine and listened to a tape of Mozart while sitting on the sofa. Mira asked me what had gone wrong with Lisa.

"Good question," I said.

"Well?"

"I don't know."

"Don't play dumb. Did you love her?"

"No," I said.

"Have you ever been in love?" she looked at me.

"No."

"Too bad," she put her wine glass down and looked away to the window. "It's excruciating while you have it. Pure torture. You pray to be released from it. And after you are, you want it back." She giggled. "It's kinda funny, wouldn't you say?"

I nodded and looked at her lean legs. She was so leggy. They were like two oars ready to push away from the shore into choppy waters.

A sweet fragrance came from her body.

"It's like losing your soul," she went on, her eyes turning back to some bittersweet experience. "You want it back so much. And you'll do anything to get it back. But it seems everything you do just ends up pushing it farther away from you."

My ears perked up. "What makes you love someone?"

She took some time. Her eyes rolled back trying to fit words to long lost feelings.

"I don't know. It could be a look in the eyes. The way they laugh. Their peculiar walk. Their smiles. And then suddenly you're toppled over. Your world is darkened. You start seeing a halo over the person's head. The light from that halo lodges itself inside you."

"Come on," I said, shaking my head.

"Yes, yes. It might not be the same for everyone. But you know when it happens. And it's painful to be away from the person you love. Because you can't breathe right. You feel a big void inside you. Your heart really hurts. Everything is dim. This is what happens, Mark. You lose the ability to live with yourself alone."

"Come on."

"Don't believe me then," she pursed her lips. "But don't say it isn't so if you've never experienced it."

"Okay, but I'd sure like to have a go at it."

"Are you making fun of me?"

"I don't think so. Let's find out."

I eased her back on the sofa. Her lips were cool and rock hard. She didn't respond.

"What's wrong?" I said.

"We shouldn't do this. Not here. Not in Lisa's place."

"Who makes up these rules?" I raised my voice. "Do girls have some sort of code? No making out in each other's apartments."

"Don't get upset," she laughed it off. "I'm just telling you I feel uneasy here. And I don't know you too well."

"Let's get to know each other," I said, cold and hard, as I eased her back again and this time put more force into my kisses. I sucked at her breath.

She was quite a handful. Strong. Hungry with desire. Smelling of bath water and newly laundered clothes. And a musky strange scent behind her ears where her wisps of hair nuzzled my nose.

"What're you doing?" she said.

"I'm smelling you," I said. "The better to eat you all up."

Sometime in our next clinch the door just behind us flew open and in walked Lisa. Like the Victory of Samothrace. Her wings fluttering.

Mira got up immediately, breaking our embrace. I was still in a daze, immobilized by delayed reaction.

"Get out," Lisa said. "The both of you."

My face felt flushed. I was speechless. I lowered my eyes and started walking out with Mira.

"Thanks, Croach," Lisa said, as I passed her. "Now you've made it so easy for me."

20

The day of our flight Lisa left the keys with the concierge. Mme Gdalia's brother came to the apartment to check things out before giving us back our deposit.

Lisa and I remained calm. All we were thinking about was getting home. The ordeal was finally over. Lisa couldn't wait to be rid of me.

We took a taxi to the airport and split the fare. Her revulsion of me came through her pores. At the check-in at Orly Lisa asked for a separate seat on the plane. I had already made arrangements for a transfer flight to the Soo. Lisa and I would split up at the airport in Toronto.

The flight was uneventful. I slept most of the time. I thought of Mira Lackovic. Bella Nardi. Janice Harcourt. Angela DiGiorgi. I read *Being and Time*.

At the airport in Toronto I tried to keep my eye on Lisa as we retrieved our luggage. She avoided me. After customs, however, she came up to me and gave me a small cardboard tube.

"What is it?" I said, avoiding her eyes.

She looked through the glass partition to the people who were awaiting the arrivals. I spotted her parents, their faces grim.

"It's something I have no further use for," she said, fussing with her luggage on the cart. "Maybe you can use it. If not, you can dump it. Have a good life, Mark."

"Wait a minute," I grabbed her arm. "You're just going

to walk away? Can't we talk for a minute? I want to explain a few things."

"No, I don't think so."

"Why not? I have some time before my flight."

"My parents are waiting. I have to go."

And she was gone.

I didn't open the tube. I was actually afraid to open it. I expected some sort of Dorian Gray portrait, all my hideous sins displayed on my face.

One September evening, though, as I was sitting on my balcony overlooking the fading light and trying to remember all the good times I had with Lisa James, I finally opened the tube.

It was a series of pencil sketches of someone sleeping from various angles. They were all very realistic, very detailed. The face could only be mine, in deep sleep, on Mme Gdalia's bed.

The sharp light of the bedside lamp illuminated only one side of my face. The other side was so shaded it was virtually obscured.

I could see every hair curled over the ears. The creases at the neck. The dark eyebrows and slight hairs on the chin.

I must've taken most of the evening looking at those sketches, trying to read what they meant. The memories of the Paris trip came flooding back. I had actually sensed her presence in the room. And dreamt it. That she was about to do me harm.

She must've sat by the bed for nights at a time, looking over me, and painstakingly trying to capture something that was worthy of capturing on a flat surface. I could picture the hard edge of the pencil being smoothed by the white paper.

The more I regarded the sketches the more the likeness looked like a child, a boy-child taking a brief respite from his journey without feet. I couldn't detect any hint of her hatred, of her rage at the turn of events. There were no boils, no deep gashes or scars, no caricatured ears or nose. The sketches were actually flattering. As if the artist in Lisa was able to see beyond her private pain and vengefulness to a clearer vision. No one had to tell me I didn't deserve such a flattering rendition of myself.

But I saw the sketches as more a portrait of Lisa than of me.

I expected some note or letter as well. But the sketches were Lisa's final word on all our time together.

I've read somewhere since that getting married is like playing musical chairs. It isn't so much a matter of love as a willingness to love. That when the time comes when you're tired of being single, that's when the music runs out, and you sit on the closest available chair.

Sometimes I see that the music had run out for Lisa much sooner than it had for me.

At other times I take out the sketches and see them in a different light. That they aren't of me at all, but of a real child that didn't exist except in Lisa's mind. Of a real child that only existed in Lisa's womb where she created things out of the pain and struggle for life. For the boy sleeping on Mme Gdalia's bed, if I look closely enough, has a high forehead and a longish face. And if he were to smile and laugh, he'd sound exactly like Lisa James.

In 1848 Kierkegaard wrote in his journal that he understood his life to be a comic drama that was only made bearable because he saw it as a martyrdom underneath. The first form of rulers were the tyrants, egotistical individuals who inhumanly ruled over the masses. But the

ever increasing worldliness of the world had displaced the
tyrants. And when the masses became the tyrant, he wrote,
then the martyr had to fight the masses. So he had to
become the suffering individual who tried to lead the
masses back into individuals.

Towards the end of his life he called himself a penitent
and a poet. He had been an ironist, a preacher, a dandy on
the surface and a melancholic underneath. He had been a
walking contradiction, as the song goes, partly truth and
partly fiction.

He had made his choice. He was no longer playing at
being this or that, the Socratic midwife. He chose his hemlock. He chose his cross. He took his leap.

And so had Lisa James.

Whereas, I . . . well, the story wasn't over.

Ever since I was a kid I had experienced these moments
of being when I seemed lifted off the ground and felt a surge
of blood like no other. This intensity of feeling I mostly felt
now in the moment of composition. It was then that I lived
most intensely. It was then that I was lost in the moment,
when time ceased, and I was no longer my little self with its
vanities and conceits and hourly deaths, but a larger Self.

After I broke up with Lisa, Kierkegaard's voice became
dimmer and dimmer. I had to go over the last conversation
I had with him in the Luxembourg. I wrote it down.

*Your outer world will always be a play. You'll always
remain a split being. An unhappy consciousness.*

Later I'd study Hegel and find out about the unhappy
consciousness. And I wouldn't understand the last statement until I found out that the Greek word for witness
also meant a martyr. I played the conversation in my mind
countless times, embellishing it, changing it to suit the
requirements of myth.

You'll always be a ghost in public, my godfather told me, walking the streets, watching TV, doing your teaching, raising your kids.

You'll always be invisible.

As for Lisa James, she did quite well. She got her degree. Then did a doctorate in New York on a famous abstract art critic. Then became a professor of art history at her former university. She had exhibitions that I went to. She began to use colour. Her life went on through a series of successes. She got involved with other men. She travelled the world. She became a spokesperson for the authentic experience. She never had children.

Every time I look at her sketches I imagine the life we could've had. The good times and the bad times that build the edifice of love between a man and a woman. I was incapable of giving her my love. But I still see her sitting beside the bed in Mme Gdalia's room drawing me in love.

It took me a long time to realize that Lisa James, in spite of herself, had chosen the cross.

I didn't choose the cross. In my own small way, I chose to serve the being inside me that trembled with fear and wonder at the darkness surrounding us.

Socrates, according to Plato, wasn't afraid of death when he chose the hemlock.

My hemlock, however, would be a slower death. And I couldn't even say I chose my hemlock. Black blood, after-all, had chosen me.

For years afterwards I looked for Lisa in every girl I saw. There was a void in me. My heart hurt terribly. My world darkened. I never re-connected with other girls. With Mira or Bella. Everything was dim. I lost the ability to live alone with myself. And I began to question what I had done, what I couldn't help doing. I had no picture of her. I never even asked for a picture of her. I could only re-create her through black blood. And let her pass over into myth.

In time the actual image I had of her was transformed into a light of great price.

True, I had thrown away that light. But at times, when I least expected it, the light flashed like an arrow in the sky and pierced the hardness of my heart.

There is more than one great paradox, I wrote down in answer to Kierkegaard.

May my moments of being with Lisa shine forever. May Lisa's spirit guide all of us.